But i Love Him

But I Love Him

AMANDA GRACE

Woodbury, Minnesota

First Edition
First Printing, 2011

Cover design by Ellen Lawson
Cover image © 2010 by Ellen Lawson

Flux, an imprint of Llewellyn Worldwide Ltd.

This is a work of fiction. Names, characters, places, and incidents are either the product of the author's imagination or are used fictitiously, and any resemblance to actual persons living or dead, business establishments, events, or locales is entirely coincidental.

Library of Congress Cataloging-in-Publication Data
Grace, Amanda
   But I love him / Amanda Grace.—1st ed.
      p. cm.
   Summary: Traces, through the course of a year, Ann's transformation from a happy A-student, track star, and popular senior to a solitary, abused woman whose love for the emotionally-scarred Connor has taken away everything—even herself.
   ISBN 978-0-7387-2594-9
[1. Abused women—Fiction. 2. Emotional problems—Fiction. 3. Interpersonal relations—Fiction. 4. High schools—Fiction. 5. Schools—Fiction. 6. Washington (State)—Fiction.] I. Title.
   PZ7.G75127But 2011
   [Fic]—dc22

                            2010050131

                               Flux
                      Llewellyn Worldwide Ltd.
                        2143 Wooddale Drive
                     Woodbury, MN 55125-2989
                          www.fluxnow.com

Printed in the United States of America

For Cyn Balog and Sarah Maas,
who are more than just writer friends,
but true friends, in every sense of the word.

August 30
ONE YEAR

I lie in pieces on the floor. A hundred different things surround me: shards of a destroyed wooden jewelry box, some cracked CDs, a few ripped books, a shredded picture of Connor and me. I think my insides must look like they do, all churned up and cracked and unrecognizable.

My lip bleeds, staining my sleeve every time I wipe my mouth. My chest is hollow and empty, as if he ripped out my heart and took it with him when he left, the door slamming so hard the picture frames crashed to the floor.

All I feel is pain, one big wave of it crashing over me again and again, relentless. I ease back on my elbows until

I'm lying flat on the ground, staring upward at the shadowy ceiling.

It's nearly dark. How long have I been lying here? The blackness reaches the corners of the room and fills everything. Once that darkness was a cocoon, enveloping us and protecting us from everything outside the door. Together, we hid in the dark, hoping the world would leave well enough alone and we could find peace.

But nothing can protect me now, least of all the darkness.

No *one* can protect me now. I pushed them all away. I lost everything. I gave it to him, and he gave me this.

I think my wrist is broken, because every time I move it, pain tears up my arm and steals my breath away.

Tonight was so much worse than anything before it. Tonight he didn't stop after the first slap. His rage spilled and bubbled and grew, and he destroyed everything he could find, and still it didn't stop.

I don't know if he left in order to find more things to break, or if it was the only thing he could do to stop it.

I don't understand how so much changed in a year, how I lost myself.

August 23

ELEVEN MONTHS, TWENTY-FOUR DAYS

Even with all the things he'd told me about his father, I'd never actually seen the monster. Sure, I'd met him many times before, but he seemed oddly human, too normal to do the things Connor told me about. The monster was a mythical thing, the villain in a twisted fairy tale.

I know right now, as I watch the flames dance and lick at that pretty white lattice, that I never fully understood it. I never really *believed* it.

I do now. It is real. And all of Connor's stories have come to life.

His father has lost his mind. His mom is sobbing, curled in a ball in the middle of their front lawn. I'm glad they live in the country, where people can't see this from the street. Otherwise I think we might all be arrested.

"I paid for this and I can tear it down!" He rips another piece of lattice off the porch. It cracks and splinters and pieces of it shower down on the flower beds. Nancy's pot of roses falls too, shattering on the cement walkway. It is just another thing he will take from her and never apologize for.

The splintered lattice goes on the roaring pile with the rest of it. The flames grow, ever skyward, gobbling everything he gives it.

Connor and I are at the edge of the yard, hidden in the shadows of the big oak tree. Jack knows we are there, but he's so lost in his own fury I think he may have forgotten. I want to grab Nancy and pull her into the shadows with us, but she's so close to him. She's begging him to stop. I don't know how she can do that; I am afraid of him.

He seems bigger today: taller, thicker, and stronger. There's something almost inhuman about him.

He has to be drunk, though he's not stumbling. A sober person wouldn't burn down their own front porch. A porch he just built a month ago. Nancy spent a whole weekend painting it, and they sat on it in lawn chairs and admired their work.

And now it's in shambles.

"Ann, you don't have to be here," Connor says, as he leans against the tree and pulls me into him. I don't reply. I just bury my face in his chest as his arms wrap around me. I can hear the wood crack and splinter as his father rips another piece from the porch. It is half gone already.

4

"Why is he doing this?" I ask.

"Why does he do anything he does?" Connor says. His voice is dull, empty. To Connor, this is an inevitable part of life, something to be endured so that he can get to the better stuff.

It was supposed to be Nancy's birthday dinner. Connor hadn't wanted to go. He doesn't like to see his father at all anymore. That was the purpose of getting his own apartment. The farther he is from his father, the better.

But for his mother, he would do anything. His mother has nothing left. I don't see her often. She's invisible most of the time. But when I do see her, I don't look her in the eyes, because they are empty. She's not yet fifty, but her hair is gray and there are deep lines in her face. There is a sadness about her that never leaves. An intensity of such deep sorrow I can't stand to be in the same room as her. She's haunted by her life, and I wonder what she is waiting for, if she will live this way forever.

If I look her in the eyes, I'm afraid I will see myself. I'm afraid I will see my future. I'm afraid of the camaraderie we may develop because of Connor and his father. And if she sees herself in me, then this is hopeless. If she looks at me and pats me on the back and just *knows* how I feel, then I'll know this is all wrong.

I will just *know.*

But Connor will not become this. Connor knows what he does is wrong. He's getting help. He promised me. We talked about it for so long, and he's going to do it now. He even brought home some information on counselors in the area. We'll work through it together, and break this cycle, and it will be because of me and because I believed in him. He's never had that before. He's never had support like I give him, and it changes him. It makes him believe in himself, too.

I won't be like everyone else. I won't abandon him when things get rough. We're both adults now—me, eighteen, him, nineteen. If we work together, the world can be ours. We won't need anyone else.

I pull away from him and look across the yard again. Darkness is falling but the blaze is growing. My little Mazda is only twenty feet away. The lawn is so dry. The fire could spread. It could burn everything.

"Do you think my car is okay?"

"Maybe."

His cheek is cool against my temple. I feel safe, wrapped up like this, even though a maniac is burning the house down one piece at a time, just a few feet away. I wonder how far he will go. Would he burn the whole house? Will he turn everything into ashes?

I know Connor is not afraid of him anymore. He told me it's been three years since his father last tried to hit him, and Connor swung back for the first time. That was the last time anything got physical between them. Connor is now three inches taller than his dad, with thicker arms and wider shoulders.

And yet his father seems so big right now.

"Do you think we should leave?"

"You can, if you want. I won't leave her."

I knew he would say that.

"He'll get bored of the porch and turn on her. But he won't do it if I'm here."

I nod. "Maybe she'll go with us."

"She won't."

And I knew that too. She cares more about her husband than herself.

I don't know what made him snap like this. The fire was already raging when we arrived, and there's too much chaos to find out what set it off.

He probably doesn't remember anyway. Rage like this doesn't answer to reason.

I can't shake the fear I feel of Jack. This isn't right. I don't think his mind is even functioning; he's just running on senseless rage. Dangerous, scary, senseless rage. It makes me anxious with fear. The tremors run up and down my legs, will me to leave this yard. I'm torn between wanting to save myself and wanting to be here for Connor.

"I think we should go," I whisper. No matter how close I get to Connor, it's not enough. I can't disappear.

"I think *you* should go. You don't need to be here for this. You don't need to see him like this. I can handle it," he says.

I nod. I know I should stay for Connor but I'm itching to get away from here, to leave this scene behind. I know it's going to haunt my dreams tonight: the hysterical sound of Nancy's sobs, the maniacal gleam in Jack's eyes, the rigid, solemn look on Connor's face. He's not shocked by what he sees.

And that's the worst part. It's the realization that this is normal to him. That it's just another day in his fucked-up life. Jack is guilty of everything Connor accuses him of. And it's making me sick. I need to get out of here. I need to lie down.

I turn away from Connor, toward my car, just as Jack yanks another chunk of lattice off the porch and flings it in the fire. The wood crackles and I jump back from a barrage of sparks, stumbling on a rock.

Jack takes offense at this. In three steps he's in front of me, his face flaming with anger, and I back up so quickly I slam into my car with a loud bang.

Connor is between us like a bolt of lightning, shouldering his dad away from me. "Don't you touch her," he says, his voice so low and menacing it makes my stomach twist into knots of dread. Connor's anger has ignited to match his father's. "Don't you *ever* touch her."

Their faces are inches apart. Time has stopped; everything is frozen. My breath has left me and I wait for it. I wait for the fists to fly and the blood to pour.

But Jack just tears his gaze away from Connor, looks over at me, and then turns back to the porch. With renewed vigor, he rips another piece loose.

It is over and I am gone. Connor kisses me quickly and then I tear out the driveway, gravel flying behind me, before I can change my mind.

———

It is nearly pitch-black in his room. The only light comes from the tiny night-light that shines into the glass heart.

I stare at it, from my place in bed. I stare until my sight blurs and all the blues and greens and amber colors blend into one mosaic.

Sometimes at night, I wake up and stare at the heart for hours, thinking of all it means to me, and to him. I think of how I worked for so long to give it to him. How I collected each piece from the beach, how I glued it all together into one big sculpture.

I wonder if he stares at it like I do. I wonder if he realizes what it means, that he'll always have a piece of me no matter what happens. Each piece of glass is another piece of myself I gave to him.

It's too bad I didn't keep any pieces for myself.

I have been lying here for hours, waiting. I know he will come back when she is safe and his father has left, and not before.

It is four a.m. when he climbs into bed beside me, and I haven't closed my eyes yet, even though they've grown so heavy it's like they're filled with sand.

I'm wearing his ratty T-shirt and boxers, and he wraps an arm around my waist once he's beside me. I pull the quilt higher so that half our faces are covered, only the tops of our heads poking out.

"I hate days like this," he says, his voice hardly above a whisper. Sometimes, when he does this, I think he's still afraid his father will hear his words. He doesn't remember that we're in his new apartment. He doesn't remember that his dad is miles away.

"I know," I say, because there are no other words.

"I wish she would just leave him."

"Me too." And I do. I wish it more than anything. It would fix everything for us. All these issues would melt away if she would just get away from him and live in peace. All the stress in Connor's life would evaporate, and then he'd be truly happy.

Silence fills the room until it is heavy. It bears down on us. It suffocates me.

"I'm sorry." The words are empty but I have to say them anyway.

"It's been a long time since he's done anything like that."

I nod.

"I'd never let him hurt you, you know."

I know that. Just as I know Jack does hurt me. He just does it through Connor's hands.

"He's held a gun to my head before," Connor says.

I've heard this story. A dozen times. But I know he will tell me again, because it is his way of getting past it. He'll talk until there is nothing else to say, and I'll listen until he falls asleep. And then it will be my turn to be haunted, my turn to toss and twist all night as I try to forget the stories and the images, to forget the way his voice will crack during the hardest parts of the story.

But the worst part of all is that I will imagine a little boy in these stories, a helpless little boy that still lives inside Connor.

"I was sitting in his truck. He went inside a Seven-Eleven. For ice cream, he said. Said he'd get me a choco-taco, my favorite."

The worst stories always come in the darkness, when I can't see his face. I can feel his breath on my neck and his arms wrapped tightly around me, like I'm his anchor. But I can never see his face.

I don't want to.

"I changed my mind. I wanted an ice cream sandwich. A fucking ice cream sandwich."

There's blame in his voice. But not for Jack. For himself. As if it's his fault, as if his dad would be someone else if only Connor didn't do things the wrong way.

"I was eight. So I got out of the truck. I pushed through the doors and the bell jingled. And my dad was standing there, a gun pointed at the clerk. When he looked over at me, the guy took his chance and swung a bat at my dad, but he missed.

"So I became his hostage. He pointed the gun at my head and told the guy to give him the money or he'd shoot me."

This is the part where he stops, where his voice cracks a little.

Tonight the story is different to me. Tonight I believe it. All these stories he's told me before, they seemed like tall tales. Exaggerations. It's not that I thought Connor would lie, it's just that I'd met Jack. He was just a regular guy. And it didn't seem like one man could be as evil as the one in the stories. That one man could cause so much pain.

But tonight I saw it, saw the monster unleashed, the one who had been there all along, and I know it is real. I know he's capable of what Connor says he is. And tonight the story comes to life in my mind, and I know the look that would have been in Jack's eyes when he did this.

"But the guy had already hit the silent alarm. The cops pulled up outside while he was standing there, jabbing at my head with the gun. It wasn't loaded, but I didn't know that."

He shifts a little. The bed creaks. He knows he doesn't have to continue, that I know the rest, but he does anyway. "It took an hour for the police to get him to drop the gun. A fucking hour.

"I was eight," he says again. "What kind of fucked-up person does it take to hold a gun to your own kid's head? They only gave him two years for it because he didn't put bullets in it. Plus parole. With good behavior he was out before I was ten."

I never have words to say, so I'm always silent. There are no words for this.

"Sometimes I wish he would have loaded it and pulled the trigger," he says.

I stiffen. I don't want our conversation to turn that direction. His anger I can handle. I can smooth out the bitter memories and hold him, and he will forget for these moments. I can do that for him; I can make the anger go away.

But his sorrow is harder. He drowns in it and I can't pull him free.

"No. I love you. Don't wish that."

And yet as I say it, the fight has gone out of me. I used to try so hard. I used to vehemently fight him. I used to struggle with everything I had to get him to stop the wars he waged with himself. I'd wipe his tears and talk to him for hours, until my eyes felt like sandpaper and I could hardly speak and I fell into an exhausted, dreamless sleep.

But I don't have it in me anymore. I'm losing him to it.

The long silence stretches between us and I wait for it. Wait to discover which way he is tipping.

"I love you too," he says, and kisses my neck.

I sigh in relief. For tonight we have won.

I turn back toward him and kiss him, and he rolls into me, kissing my cheeks and lips and chin and neck, and in seconds we are lost to it.

These are the only moments we have left. These precious seconds where the passion blots out everything else, and it is just us. The rest is a war neither of us can ever win.

But I have already waved my white flag.

I have already surrendered.

August 15

ELEVEN MONTHS, SIXTEEN DAYS

I've made a mistake. A huge, monumental mistake.

I forgot Connor's truck broke down. I forgot he was going to be waiting for me when I walked out of Subway. I've only been back on the job for two weeks, and it's already putting a strain on my relationship with Connor.

And now he's seen me. He's seen me laugh and push Mark, the new guy.

And I know what he's thinking, and I know where his mind is going, and I know without asking that he's *steaming*, waiting for me. I know the fear he has of losing me overpowers everything else, even his common sense. I know deep inside he trusts me, but I know his raging insecurities will always prevail.

He's so afraid of losing me that he can't see I'd never leave him.

And I know he had to have seen the way Mark hugged me with one arm, just a loose sideways hug, but still a hug. He won't believe me when I say Mark means nothing. He'll just replay that hug over and over in his mind and he'll spin a story that's so far from the truth.

I've been so careful for so long. It was bound to happen eventually. I was bound to slip and do something like this. Why do I even wonder why I have no friends anymore? Why do I even wonder why no one talks to me? It's my own doing. It's my own fears that something will happen and I'll say the wrong thing to the wrong person, and they'll interfere somehow. And this is what will happen.

Even Abby knows it. It's why she stays away without me telling her to. It's why she smiles that sad smile when she sees me.

It's why she's stopped trying to be my friend. She was the last to give up. The last to surrender me to Connor.

I hate this. I hate it so much, this waiting as we walk toward my car, Mark having no idea what's about to happen and me knowing it too well.

I'm afraid. I hate that I'm actually afraid of him right now. I hate that I know what this silence means, and all I can do is wait for it to explode.

I feel claustrophobic and I'm not even in the car yet. I consider running. Away from him, away from everything.

I could go five, ten miles before I had to stop. I'd be half-way to Aberdeen by then. Our tiny ocean town of Westport, Washington, is a town of nothing. I'd be gone in ten minutes.

But that won't solve it, and maybe this time he'll talk to me. He's been getting a little better, now that he's away from his dad so much. He's been cooling. Adjusting. Maybe this time he'll understand, and he'll see that Mark is just some random guy who means nothing at all, and we can use this to grow from.

I know that's going to happen, if I stick with him long enough. He just needs some guidance, some love, some understanding. He wants *so* badly to become that person.

But of course that's not the case. When he clicks his door shut, and before I start the car, he grabs my wrist and squeezes, too hard. It's always too much, too intense, too everything.

"Forget the store. Take me to the apartment. Now."

And for some reason, the whole ride there, the whole deathly silent ride, I keep hoping that my car will break down too and I'll have to get out, that we'll never make it to his apartment.

But we do. I pull up at his fourplex, parking so carefully, perfectly between the white lines. I stare at the other three doors, hoping no one is home in those apartments. It's a tiny building, two apartments downstairs, two up. Connor's is on the upper left, with a big crooked number three nailed to the door.

I follow him up the old wooden stairs, my heart pounding. I can hardly feel the thin railing as it slides underneath my hand, guiding me toward the front door with the peeling red paint.

We're barely through the entry before he shoves me, hard, and I'm sent sprawling all over the floor. I bang my elbow and a jolt of electricity shoots up my arm. I hear the door slam behind me, and the pictures on the wall rattle with the force.

I lie there longer than I should, trying to keep my breathing down, trying to suppress the instinct to curl in a ball. I know his moods can turn with the right words. I know if I think clearly, I can steer him back toward being himself again.

If I do this right, Connor will be back.

"You're such a slut," he says, spitting the words at me. "Do you spread your legs for him, too?"

I'm stunned into silence. He's been cruel before…but this…this is coming from somewhere deeper.

"*No,* God, no. I love you. Only you."

I hardly cry anymore when he's like this. I've become numb to it, and the tears don't come like they used to. I just take it and wait, and when it's over I hold him until he is through hating himself for this, and we pretend it never happened.

But today the tears are brimming at his words. They bruise so much deeper than his fist.

"You're so fucking stupid, you know that? How could you think he would look twice at you once he has you?

I'm the one who'll stick with you. Who keeps you around. You're nothing to him."

That can't be all I am to him. He can't be just "keeping me around." He needs me. Just as I need him. But hearing the words buckles everything inside of me. I fold in on myself and bury my face in my knees and wrap my arms around my legs and try to disappear. I could drown in my own tears.

He hauls me up off the ground, sending waves of pain up my shoulder at the way he jerks me. Then he backs me into a wall, so he has me cornered.

He always does it like this. It's like he wants me to be trapped. It ensures I never leave until his anger is gone. It ensures he can always fix the things he's ruined instead of letting me walk out the door with an ugly feeling swirling in my stomach.

I can never walk away with this image in my mind. It is always the aftermath, the tears in his eyes, the begging for forgiveness. But it's getting messier and more complicated every day. It's getting harder to remember the apologies before the hits.

Not when they're coming more often. Not when the sweet spots are shrinking and the anger is boiling and nothing is going the way I thought it would.

Why? Why does he have to let his anger explode like this?

How does he look at me like this, trembling, crying, and continue to yell? How can he look me in the eyes and be so cruel?

I could never do this to him. Never.

"You have no idea how fucking stupid you are."

And then he reels back, his hand fisted, and punches.

The wall.

It caves in around me, bits of drywall showering down around my shoulders.

And that is that.

The first hit, the first good, hard hit, usually wakes him up. I can actually see it in his face, this abrupt before and after.

I always know when it shifts. I think maybe the pain, so raw and real, pulls him out of his rage. Today I am lucky. Today it is the wall, and not me.

He blinks, twice, and looks at me. At the way I tremble in front of him.

"Oh. I…" He steps away from me. There is always a moment like this. A moment where I think he is seeing himself, where he's reeling everything back inside him, forcing it back down and bottling it back up, and then he turns to me. For that split second before he gains his senses again, I see that same shock and fear on his face as must be mirrored on mine. I see that he has no idea what he's done. That he had no control of himself.

But it's not fair. It's not fair that he lets his rage take over, that he lets it rule him. I don't know why he has to be two people.

I don't know why he *gets to be* two different people, and I only get to be me, the one who is here to take what he has to give, and who is here to pick up the pieces afterward.

Me. It's always me. I don't want it to be like this anymore. I can't handle more of this. I'm barely holding it together.

I'm barely holding *him* together.

It's just not fair.

He steps forward to hug me, but I stiffen and he has to force his arms around me to get the hug to work.

And I let out a sob of relief, because it's over. The episode is over. Today he didn't touch me. And I think this may be a good thing, it may mean he's not going to. Ever again. If he can see me with another guy and get this angry and not touch me, it has to mean something. I let myself hope that it means something, because otherwise I'm not sure how much longer I can last.

He holds me and I melt into a mess of sobs, which shocks me. I thought I was done doing this. I thought I could steel myself from this. But I can't handle the roller coaster anymore. I can't handle this up and down.

He lets me slide to the floor and then he pulls me into his lap and he rocks me, back and forth, as I sob so hard I can't breathe and start hiccupping.

"I'm sorry, Ann. I'm so sorry."

I sniffle, my breath coming out in funny little rasps. "I don't want you to be sorry. I want you to stop doing this. I want it to be like it was when we met."

"I know. It will be, I promise. I'll treat you like I used to. I swear."

I nod my head, wanting to believe it.

But even when I stop crying, even when we fall asleep and I'm nestled in his arms, this will leave another scar. No one will see it. No one will know. But it will be there. And eventually all the scars will have scars and that is all I will be, one big scar of a love gone wrong.

July 30
ELEVEN MONTHS

'm oddly nervous. Today, I'm unveiling my sculpture, and I desperately want him to see it and finally understand how much I love him. I want him to *feel it*, to the depth of his soul, like I do.

He is late getting home, and I pace the floors near the window, waiting to see the headlights smear across the wall. When they finally do, I practically jump out of my skin.

I wait near the front door, a soft smile on my lips, as he ascends the stairs, his steel-toed boots pounding on each step. With each footfall, my nerves intensify, until they are nearly buzzing up and down my arms and legs.

"Hey sweetheart," I say, and reach out to kiss him.

"Hi." His voice is gruff and he's barely touched his lips to mine before he's moving past me, like he hasn't even seen me at all.

"I made you something," I say.

"I'm not hungry." He passes down the hall and disappears into the bathroom before I can respond. I stare after him for a moment, the front door still ajar behind me.

I follow him. "It's not food, it's—"

"I got fired, Ann. I'm not in the mood for chit-chat, okay?"

It's hard not to step back at the sound in his voice. There's a dangerous edge to it. An edge that tells me to stay away. Far, far away. If I were smart, I would leave. Right now, before it grows, before it simmers and stews and explodes.

It was bound to happen, of course. He was often so tired he probably didn't work at all. Not on the nights he was up late, helping his mom. Not on the nights he tossed and turned, so tortured by his past he didn't care about the future.

He missed some days. He was late. And yet somehow I didn't see it coming.

Now what? Do I hide the heart? Save it for a better day? It's sitting on the dining room table in all its shimmering glory, under the glow of the chandelier. I don't know where I'd put it even if I wanted to move it. I could toss a sheet over it, maybe. Hope he doesn't notice it.

When I hand that beautiful piece of art to him, I want

him to smile. I want to *see* the impact it has on him as he stares at it, knowing how much I love him.

And none of that will happen if he's in this kind of mood. All those hours and hours of work will be for nothing. I can't let that happen. It has to be for a reason. I have to see the payoff, or the disappointment will just be too much to bear.

I nod to myself and head toward the hallway closet. We must have some spare sheets or something. Or maybe the whole closet is big enough. I could make a little area on a shelf, put it up there where it is safe. It's not much bigger than a basketball, though oddly shaped and far more fragile.

I dig around in the closet, trying to move some towels and boxes, desperate to find enough room for it before Connor leaves the bathroom. He's not in the mood for a gift. He might react strangely to it. I need to save it for a better day. A better opportunity. A better—

"What is this?"

His voice carries down the hall. He's not in the bathroom at all. He's in the dining room. My heart throws itself around in my chest. It's too late to hide it.

I walk toward him, praying he's happy, praying all those months were for something. When I round the corner and see his face, the nervous rigidity in my limbs melts away.

His face has softened, and his eyes are expressing a gratitude I've never seen before. They shine with it. He walks over to me, wraps his arms around me, and rests his chin on the top of my head. "Thank you. I needed this today. *Really* needed it."

I nod and rest my cheek against his chest. I can hear his heart beat, calm and rhythmic, and it soothes me until we are both so relaxed we just sort of melt to the floor and keep hugging.

"I love you," he says. "I'll always love you."

"So you like it?" I ask, pulling back to see his eyes.

"Yes. I love it. It's beautiful."

I grin. "I'm glad. I've been working on it for months. I collected all the glass myself, from the beach."

"It means so much to me. You have no idea. I'll treasure it always. Just like you."

I smile and hug him again. I've done well.

Finally, I've done well.

August 30

ONE YEAR

Every piece of my body throbs. It pulses up and down my legs and arms and radiates outward from my chest. I sit up and try to shift my weight, hoping to find a part of me that doesn't feel bruised and sore, but the glass scattered around me crunches under my weight, and I stop.

It's shattered. The whole beautiful sculpture. It's in a thousand pieces around me, littering the floor, each tiny piece symbolizing another hour I spent searching out the sea glass, painstakingly assembling it with all of its mates.

And now it's nothing. Just like me.

I reach up toward the bed and pull the ratty orange quilt off the mattress, covering myself completely. Now and then, the lightning strikes and my cocoon takes on a russet glow. The room buzzes with the sounds of the pouring rain, but I welcome it. It fills the room and drives away the silence.

A burst of light comes from the window, and the flash glints off a piece of tumbled amber glass poking into my cocoon. I kick it swiftly away. I can't ignore the ache in my chest as I watch it disappear. He knew how much that sculpture meant. He knew the nights I stayed up late putting it together.

He told me he would treasure it always.

Instead, he threw it in an explosion of rage.

The air inside the blanket warms, and I rock back and forth, back and forth, inside this bubble where nothing exists but me.

I don't know what to do anymore.

I am alone.

Just as he intended.

July 16

TEN MONTHS, SIXTEEN DAYS

Why can't you just hate me?" He's not looking at me. He's sitting in a chair, staring at his hands. I know he's studying the white lines that criss-cross his skin. They line his knuckles like a road map, evidence of where he's come from. "Why can't you just see you're too good for me?"

"I'm—"

"Yes, you are! And you know you are!"

I hate these times. I hate when he tries to convince me to leave him. He doesn't want me to. I know he doesn't. But I also know he feels guilty for what he does. It eats him alive.

I know there are days he wishes he would wake up without me and I would be gone forever, and he could imagine me happy. Some days I think that would do more for him than I can do when I'm with him.

But it's too late for that, because I could never leave. I know the truth. I know he would never make it without me here, picking up the pieces, pushing him in the right direction. I have to fix everything. I have to tape it all together and cover up the cracks and hope no one notices that nothing is ever as good as new.

"Please," I say. "Don't do this today, okay? Just come here. Just hold me."

Sitting on the bed, I hold my hands up, toward him, like a mother would to a child. But he doesn't move toward me, and I just end up sitting there, my arms achingly empty.

"No. You need to listen to me this time. You need to just go and forget about me and never look back." He looks down at me, his eyes shining with tears he won't shed. "There are a thousand reasons we will never work and you know it. It's time to face it."

I stare back at him, at those thick lashes framing his intense blue eyes. His blond hair is matted with yesterday's gel.

He can't take my staring and turns away, rubbing his neck as he sighs.

"But I love you," I say, the first tears brimming. One finally rolls down my cheek.

"You can do so much better than this." His voice is

nearly a whisper, but it's still full of conviction. He believes what he is saying, and he wants me to believe it too.

"Please," I say.

"No," he says, louder. He looks down at me again, stares straight into my eyes. "I'm going. I'll just get in my car and drive and I'll end up wherever I end up, and I'll start over. I won't miss you. I won't think of you. And you'll be so much better without me."

I'm shaking my head so fast the tears land everywhere.

"Stop crying," he says.

"I can't!"

"It doesn't fix anything."

I bury my face in my knees and sob, big choking gasps that rack my body. I can't breathe. The tears are stealing the air and life away from me.

I can't live without him. I don't know who I am anymore if I'm not Connor's girlfriend. Doesn't he see that's all I am now? Doesn't he see that I've given up everything for him? That I didn't apply to college, that I gave up my friends, that I picked him over my mom?

Doesn't he get that I exist for him?

"How can you do this to me?" I say. I try to look up at him through my tears, but I can't see him. He's swimming in them. "Why do you always do this and hurt me? I don't do this to you."

"I have to. You have to leave. You don't understand this. I'm never going to be the person you want me to be."

"But you *are* the person I want you to be!"

"That's a lie," he says, practically spitting the words.

And it is. I know it is. I know the person I see only exists in tiny little scenes. I know it's not the whole Connor. He's still ruled by things his dad has done, by the past he has lived, by his anger. It will be a long time before he's really the person I know he can be.

I gasp for air. It's not coming fast enough. My lungs are inflating but it's not enough. I can't breathe.

He seems to realize what I'm doing and all at once he's beside me on the bed, pulling me to him, into his lap, until his arms are around me. I turn to him and bury my face in his shoulder. His shirt is wet with my tears.

"I need you. Please, I need you." I don't know if he understands my words. I can hardly hear them through my tears. The lump in my throat makes it too hard to speak.

"I'm sorry. Don't cry. It's okay. Just don't cry."

I don't know how long we sit like that, him rocking me and whispering in my ear. My sobs continue until I'm empty of them.

"Shh. I'm sorry. I'm so sorry. Don't cry. I love you. Please, please don't cry." He rocks me and rubs my back, and I can finally breathe again. His other hand is stroking my hair, soothing and soft. "Please, shhh. I love you. I love you I love you I love you."

I inhale several long, slow breaths, and my tears slow enough that I can blink them back. "I need to blow my nose," I say, my voice bloated and raspy.

He reaches over to his dresser and hands me a big fluffy white towel. I blow three times before I can get any air in through my nose. Even when I do, it rattles through the snot.

We fall back against the bed and he pulls me closer to him, wrapping himself around me until I can't tell where I end and he begins. I don't want to know anymore. I want us to be the same person.

His room is dark, like it always is. The sounds of the radio fade away until all I hear is his breathing mixed with mine.

It's just us again, calm and quiet. He grabs the blankets and pulls them up around us, and I nestle closer.

I'm so tired of this. I'm exhausted to my bones. The pain is even deeper. The fear that one day he will truly leave. That he will think he's doing me a favor. I feel as if I'm falling down a mountain, clawing at anything I can grab, and I'm missing everything and picking up speed, and eventually there will be a cliff, and I will have nothing.

"I'm sorry I do this to you," he whispers.

"Yes," I say, because that's all I can manage. I have no energy for more words. My eyes are closed and heavy.

"I don't want to be like this anymore. I want to be happy."

I don't respond because I'm falling now, sleep is coming. He doesn't seem to mind, he just turns his face into my hair and breathes deeply. The smell of his cologne washes over me like a lullaby.

And we fall asleep like that. Holding on so tight our arms ache.

July 6

TEN MONTHS, SIX DAYS

There was a note on my windshield today. I saw it as I walked up to my car. It made me grin. He used to leave me notes everywhere, in my jacket pockets and on my car and inside my books. But it has been weeks since his last one.

You're so beautiful to me.

I smile and tuck the note into my pocket. I keep them all. They fill a box in the closet, and I often take them out and filter through his words.

When I arrive at his apartment I know he's in a good mood. I used to make him this happy all the time. He could be a ball of stress and nerves when I showed up, and

I could soothe him. It's what made me special. And I'm not like his mom—I don't *have* to be there like she does. I choose to. And that's what makes a difference. I choose him and I love him, and he knows it.

But that rarely works anymore. I don't know why. I don't know when I stopped mattering to him, and I don't know how to undo it. I want it to be like it used to, when all he needed was me.

Today he cooked me dinner and bought me flowers, and we eat in front of the television as an old Tom Hanks movie plays out on the screen.

It's cozy. He laughs at the movie, his voice bubbling up, a smile breaking through and lighting up his eyes. He is the Connor I fell in love with. I want to laugh with him, but I don't have it in me. I think my laughter might be broken, like everything else inside me. If he looks at me, I will fake it, because I want him to stay happy.

He sets his fork down on the edge of his plate and slips his arm around me, and I melt into him. I rest my face against his chest and hear his heart beat steadily.

If I close my eyes, I can lose myself and slip away from everything. These moments are like islands in a stormy sea, and I take them and hide and hope that no one ever finds me. I want to be the castaway, like Tom Hanks, forgotten on my private little island.

He rests his chin on the top of my head. "I love you," he says.

He says it a lot. I think he worries that I will forget.

But I still don't think he loves me as much as I love

him. I'm desperate for him to understand. I *need* him to understand. If he knew, he wouldn't feel like he does. He'd know he can take on the world, he'd know we are unstoppable together. He'd know it's us against them.

Soon, he *will* understand, because the sculpture is almost done. The glue has to cure for a few more days. And then I will give it to him, and then he'll finally see.

"Do you want to go for a walk?" he asks.

The movie isn't over, but I nod anyway. We've seen this film a half-dozen times because it's one of Connor's favorites.

He hands me his jacket, the one I always wear. I slip it over my shoulders and push my arms into the sleeves. They're big and warm. I feel good inside it, like it's a coat of armor. He never wears jackets. He never feels cold, I guess.

His apartment complex is small, so we're out of the lot in thirty seconds, walking down the road. The wet pavement sparkles under the streetlamps, a mid-summer rain that can't dampen our mood.

We walk hand-in-hand through the little residential neighborhoods, past all the broken-down cars and ugly chain-link fences. A pit bull growls at us, but Connor just flips it off. I don't know why he does that. It's not like the dog cares.

Eventually, the houses get bigger. The fences become wood. The cars get shinier. We're back to the land of the privileged, the ones who have no idea the kinds of things that go on behind closed doors. I once belonged to this world, but I don't think it ever belonged to me.

And then before we can get lost in our walk, like we usually do, I see *him*, and my heart leaps into my throat and I can't breathe.

Everything around him fades and all I see is him, and I know he sees us, because he is just standing next to his car, frozen, one hand still on the door. He stares straight at me, as if he's caught in headlights. As if we won't see him if only he doesn't move.

He knows what will happen if Connor sees him. Just as I know.

How did I not notice that we'd drifted into his neighborhood? How could I be so stupid as to bring Connor here?

"Let's, um, let's go this way," I say, tugging on Connor's arm. He can't see him. Not tonight. Not when everything is going so well and I just want to be with him and I just want the drama to stop and I just want to forget that everything is so fucked up. I just want to walk in the darkness and forget all this and now I can't.

Because Connor sees Blake. He sees him and he's letting go of my hand and walking straight at him. I recognize his posture. It's gone rigid. His shoulders are square, his hands are in fists. His strides are long and purposeful. I know every muscle in his body is tense. Ready.

And I know what's coming.

It's Connor who takes the first swing. Blake goes down, sprawling across the concrete that I'd thought looked so pretty with fresh rain just moments before.

But it's not rain on the road anymore. It's blood.

I fall to my knees, just as Blake has. All these months of protecting him. All this time playing peacekeeper and martyr and smoothing out the edges of the conversations and downplaying everything and avoiding Blake and never once mentioning his name.

And it's over, and they're fighting.

But Blake doesn't go down that easily. He gets back up and I hear the *crack* his fist makes as it connects with Connor's chin. I see him in a way I've never seen him. *Angry.* And I know it's because of me. I know all these months that Blake's wanted this, he's wanted to take Connor and shake him and scream at him and make him see what he's done to me.

All those times I stood in front of him, those words swam in his eyes, but none of them were spoken. And now it has come to this. This is what I've caused.

A porch light flicks on and someone's door creaks open. A man's voice shouts out.

A car alarm goes off when Connor backs up and falls half onto the hood. He kicks Blake in the leg and Blake grunts with the pain, keeling over, gripping his shin. Shadows dance under the streetlight as they spar.

I crawl to the stop sign beside me and use it to drag myself off the street.

And then I run. I turn away from them both, away from the sounds. My feet pound on the concrete. There is no air in my lungs to run like this, but my legs don't want to stop. My years of cross country and track have developed muscles that yearn to race like they once did, so I don't stop. Connor's jacket flies out behind me like a cape, the zipper rattling in the wind.

I don't go back to our apartment. I run straight past it and keep going, away from town, toward the country roads. I run past the elementary school and its swing sets and slides. I run alongside ditches filled with trash and cattails.

I run until I collapse in front of my mom's house.

But I haven't outrun anything. It will catch me. There is no escaping who I am now.

I sit on the front lawn, my legs crossed, staring at the dark house. My mom's bedroom window faces this lawn, but I know she's not awake. It's well past midnight, now. I must have run for over an hour.

I wonder what she would think if she knew I was here. If she could see how broken I am inside. If she could see the faded bruises on my shoulders where he grabbed me last. If she knew the haunted world I live in, she would lock me away and never let me see him again, even if that meant I hated her forever.

That house is not home anymore, but I ache for it anyway. I want to open the door and ascend the stairs and fall into a bed where nothing can get me, where I will sleep for hours and not dream. My chest throbs with the desire to do it—to cross the lawn and pick up the hidden key and slip inside the door and lock it behind me, and never answer it again.

I want to wake up and eat pancakes and talk about going to the mall and my next cross-country meet. I want my mom to tell me the last crazy thing Grandma said, and I want to laugh at it.

I want to sit in her kitchen and bathe in the light. I want to help her plant flowers in the spring and bulbs in the fall. I want to watch one of her horrible black and white movies and whine the whole time about how boring it is until she hands me the remote and I make her watch *America's Next Top Model* instead.

I want my dad to come back and make everything okay again, like he did when I was little. He'd swoop in and fix my Barbies and my flat bicycle tires. He could fix anything.

I wonder if he could fix this.

The shadows of the trees dance in a breeze. I try to remember who I was the last time I was in that house, but I can't. I can remember the things, but I can't remember me. I don't know the old me anymore. She was smiley and bubbly and outgoing. She had everything; the world was at her feet.

I wish I could have it both ways. I wish I could be there for him and help him and be the one he needs me to be, and still be that other person, too. But I can't, and I can't live without him, either.

And he would drown in himself if I left him.

I know he's waiting. I know that his face is probably swollen, and that he will need me. I know I will have to call in sick for him tomorrow and help him ice his new black eye, and we will have to come up with a way of explaining it.

I don't know when it stopped being what it was, when

it became something else. When it became *this*. It wasn't this way in the beginning. It was beautiful and passionate and filled with things I've never felt before. Things I want back so desperately I can taste it.

I don't want this anymore; I don't want this horrible whirlpool of constant emotion, churning and bubbling at every turn. And yet I feel as if I don't know any other life—like the other seventeen years never existed. I feel like I was born into this.

I get up and walk away from the house. It is too big for me; it stands over me, leaving me in the shadows, and I can't sit here anymore.

I turn toward the street and begin the descent back toward town, toward Connor and his apartment. In the distance, the ocean sparkles under the full moon, until the clouds shift and blot out the light.

I glance back one more time as my house disappears behind me. The house I grew up in, the house full of so much laughter.

I don't know what happiness feels like anymore.

I am dead to it.

June 12

Today is graduation. I don't know how I made it this far. I don't know why they are giving me a diploma. But I'm proud, because I have done it. And I deserve it after this year.

He's out there somewhere. He's proud of me too.

But I still feel alone. I wonder if my mom knows the ceremony is today. I wonder what she would have said if I'd asked her to come.

She would have been surprised, but I bet she would have liked it.

My classmates surround me as I sit in this folding chair. They laugh and hug one another and talk about how much they will miss each other once they're gone. And all I can think is that I have been gone for a long time, but none of them miss me.

I know Abby is somewhere behind me, with the other R's and S's, and I can't stop wondering if she's looking at me. I can't stop wondering if she even cares who I am anymore. I want to turn around and look for her. I want to turn around and look *at* her. But if she gives me the kind of look the rest of these people do, the look that says they forgot I even went here, it will kill me.

I don't look in Blake's direction, either, though I can guess where he's sitting in the sea of other purple graduation caps and gowns. I haven't seen him since the street fair last week.

Since the disaster last week.

One of my classmates is standing at the microphone, blasting a pearly white smile at all of us. She's talking about the future and possibilities and how we can dream of anything we want and it will become ours.

That's not true. For some people, their destinies are decided when they are little. For some people, they don't get a chance at a future. They only get darkness and a stolen childhood. And it ruins everything, forever.

It goes on for hours, or so it seems. Name after name. Flashbulbs and cheers. I wonder if they all think this is a big deal. I wonder if they think this is some life-changing moment, if it actually means anything at all.

It doesn't. It's a piece of paper.

When my row stands, I almost stay where I am. I'm

not one of them anymore. It feels wrong to follow Veronica Masterson and Vic Mathews. I don't belong here.

When it's my turn, I walk to the podium and reach out to take the roll of paper. The principal nods toward the camera guy and he takes our picture.

I don't smile.

Just as I'm about to walk away, back to my seat, I see her.

My mom. She's staring at me with intense blue eyes. Her dark hair is spilling over her forehead, casting shadows on her face, but I know she's looking right at me. We lock eyes. She's here. I can't believe she's here. Watching me. Supporting me, like she once did from the stands at my track meets.

I freeze. I have not spoken to her in at least a month, and it was a short, awkward phone call. She hasn't tried calling since.

We are strangers. And yet she's here. That has to mean something. I have to mean something to her.

The principal nudges me into motion and the moment is broken, and I walk away, but I can still feel her eyes on me, following me.

Why is she here? Does she want to talk to me? Does she want to take me home, away from Connor?

I want to get out of here. I don't want her to find me afterwards and try to convince me to leave him. I don't want to listen to that same conversation, over and over. I don't want to defend myself and defend him. It takes too much out of me. Even I know my words sound empty and stupid and that I'll never convince her.

She'll never understand him. She'll never understand us. I hate the voice she uses when she talks about him.

I can't hear it today.

I follow a stream of people back to my row but when they turn, I just keep walking. People are staring at me. They are whispering. They want to know what I'm doing, but I don't say anything. They'd never understand if I told them anyway.

I just keep walking, past the last rows and to the back of the auditorium. When I push through the exit doors, the sun is so bright I have to shut my eyes. I stumble over the curb and land on my knees in the grass. Bile rises up before I know it and I puke in the grass, right next to the doors. Tears sting my eyes as my throat burns with it.

Connor finds me. He always does. He pulls my hair away from my face and waits in silence for me to put myself back together. He is so used to a world of pain that he always knows how to respond, always knows when to talk and when to stay silent.

"Let's get out of here," I say. I don't want the world to see me like this. I don't want them to know what I've been reduced to.

He helps me to my feet and we leave while the auditorium erupts in applause.

That is not reality. This is reality.

This is my reality.

June 6

There's a street fair in town today, along the boardwalks and the marinas. Connor and I go there so we can have candied apples and stroll up and down the sidewalks looking at things we won't buy, but we'll spend all day doing it anyway. Days like these are perfect. They're just lazy and they don't seem real, like for a day we step outside ourselves and pretend we're other people.

It's sunny today, the first real hot day of summer. I can't wait to spend the rest of it with him. I don't know what I'll do with myself, but I'll do something, so long as I can stay with Connor during every free moment.

Connor gets lost in a display of baseball cards, and I

wander down to a booth displaying dozens of oil paintings. They're gorgeous. Horses and cows and mountains and the ocean—paintings of every natural beauty I can imagine. I get lost staring at them; the real world fades behind me as I study their bright colors.

But it all turns gray when I hear his voice.

"Hey, stranger."

Blake. My heart jumps into my throat at the sight of him, but I don't know if it's because I haven't seen him in so long or if it's because I know Connor is just feet away, his back to us.

He looks good, a baseball cap over the dark hair that brings out his expressive brown eyes. As I stare at him, I think of that day we ran in the forest. I think of that moment, and I play it over and over again as I stare at him and try to keep the panic at bay.

"Hi. Um, it's not a good time, okay?"

I whisper it. I sound ridiculous. Even I know that.

And he knows why I'm acting like this, because he stands up straighter and looks in all directions, scanning the crowd for his rival.

Connor turns around, as if on cue, and meets his gaze. I see the way his hands slip off the baseball cards he was flipping through and now shoves hard into his pockets as he walks over to us, his quick long strides gobbling up the ground before I can think of a way out of this.

"What the hell do you think you're doing?" Connor says, his voice loud. *Too* loud. I know the other fair-goers hear him. I see their stares without meeting their gaze.

Judging me. Everyone wants to judge me.

"Nothing, man. Just talking to an old friend."

"I told you to stay away from her," Connor says.

Blake arches one eyebrow. He looks equal parts irritated and amused, as if Connor isn't a threat to him. "Last I checked, you don't control what I do."

My face drains of all blood even though my heart is pounding so hard I can barely make out their words. I start to step closer to them, to come between them, but Connor blocks me as he moves in front of me. Does he think he is protecting me from Blake? Or from his own fists if he chooses to throw them?

"Fuck off, buddy," Connor says. He has a few inches on Blake, but I know Blake is in the best shape of his life. I can see it on him, all the muscle, taut over his arms and legs as he clenches his fist, looking more defensive than aggressive.

"I don't want trouble," Blake says. I know it's the truth. I know Blake has no interest in a fist fight. "I just want to talk to her."

"Talking time is over."

Blake takes one step back, but that's it. It's a compromise Connor won't accept. Connor doesn't do compromise.

"You have no idea what you're doing to her," Blake says. "You're taking everything from her."

"I'd say that's none of your fucking business."

Blake makes this groan in the back of his throat, like he's trying hard to suppress the urge to reel back and sock

Connor in the face. I'm surprised by it. Surprised Blake possesses that kind of fury. But then Blake gets that sad look again and shakes his head. "You're crushing her. Don't you get it? She was a different person before she met you."

I sit down on the curb because I can't handle this anymore, and I don't want people to think I'm with them. I don't like the pity in people's eyes or the curious looks as they slow their pace so they can gobble up the drama, like this is some fun television show and not my fucked-up reality.

Connor puts his hands out to shove Blake, but Blake steps away before he connects, which makes Connor stumble. I know Connor is holding back. I know he realizes this is a public place and he can't unleash the anger he's bottling inside.

They're close to cutting loose. *So* close. They dance around like boxers, but neither of them touches the other.

"What made you do this to her? What do you say to yourself to make it okay?"

"You don't know what you're talking about," Connor says, his voice growing darker, deeper, every time he speaks. Blake is pushing all the right buttons. I can't believe Connor hasn't lost it yet.

"You're turning her into something else. If you love her, you won't do this anymore. You'll let her go so she can get on with her life."

"Fuck off," Connor says.

Blake just stares straight at him and shakes his head, a slow, sad shake that seems to last forever. "You'll lose her eventually and you'll know I was right. You'll know she's above you." He turns and looks at me. "You have a choice. You're better than this."

And then he turns and leaves me with Connor.

He leaves me with the mess he's so carelessly made.

And for one second, I actually think I might run after him. I actually think I might leave Connor here to just get over it on his own.

But then I look at Connor again and I remember all those whispered promises and all those times I swore I'd always be there to pick up the pieces, to always help him keep everything together, and I don't.

I promised him. Forever and always.

I promised.

May 31

NINE MONTHS, ONE DAY

With my high school career unofficially complete, I become listless. Classes are over but the graduation ceremony hasn't been held yet, and I haven't picked up any shifts at Subway, my usual summer job. Connor is at work, and I end up wearing my running shoes, a windbreaker, and track pants. My iPod is turned on full blast and I'm ready to leave every shred of stress behind.

It's windy today and the surf is frothy with foam, each wave breaking violently as it nears the shore. Seagulls bob along the surface and the sand is littered with debris.

It's a perfect day to find sea glass. There is so much on the shore that I decide to run a few miles first and pick it up on my way back, or I won't even be able to raise my heart rate.

I run along the wet section of the sand, where it's firm, and leave my footprints behind as I pick up a full sprint. I shouldn't push so hard so quickly; I should warm up and stretch and take my time. But I don't want to.

It's been so long since I've been able to run. It's been so long that the passion has been buried down inside me, twisted up and hidden until I tried to pretend I never ran at all. But as soon as my muscles warm and my breathing picks up that familiar rhythm, everything starts to float away.

Why did I stop doing this? Why did I give it up?

Connor wants me to be happy. He would understand if I told him I was leaving to go for a run. He'd probably encourage it, if I told him what it meant. But somehow something more important is always in the way.

No more. I want to run like this every day. I'll wake up at four a.m. if I have to. I want it back.

I want *me* back.

I run much further than I'd planned to, until the fine yellow sand turns rockier and a big jetty extends out into the water. I turn away from the waves and circle back, slowing to a walk as I pant for air. Adrenaline courses through me.

I feel confident. Alive. How did I forget all this?

———

Back at Connor's, I empty out the canvas bag onto the work bench in the little garage. I have at least a few dozen pieces of glass, in blue and green and amber. Enough to finish my project. It's been so hard to find the time to work on it. I thought I'd be done months ago.

I put on rubber gloves and then sort out the glass, putting it into little piles based on size and color. I need small pieces for the spots where the sculpture curves, and then bigger pieces in the large flat spots.

I pick up the bottle of glue and a little red piece. I have three hours before Connor will be back. If I'm lucky I can finish it and give it to him in a couple days, after the glue cures. He would like that. He needs a pick-me-up these days.

I reach over and flick on the radio, and an upbeat country song blasts out. I hum along as I pick up another piece.

Yes, I will finish this today. It has taken eight months of work, and it has grown along with my love for Connor, a physical symbol of how I feel for him. Finally, he will understand how much I love him. He will *see* it.

And then he'll know that I mean it when I say I'll never leave him.

May 28

EIGHT MONTHS, TWENTY-EIGHT DAYS

I can barely stay awake today. Connor had a bad night last night. His mom called, freaking out, but when he went to her house, no one was home. And he spent the rest of the night worrying about her. I didn't sleep at all.

I'm leaning on my hand, my hood pulled as far over my eyes as possible, when something drops onto my desk.

Note cards. Dozens of them, with a neat little scrawl filling the lines.

Abby's handwriting.

I look up to see her staring at me, her eyes empty of all emotion.

"Just read everything on the pink cards. The yellow ones are mine."

Then she walks away and takes her seat near the front, and all I can do is stare at her.

Our project. Our year-long, *half-of-your-final-grade* senior project.

I've spent maybe a dozen hours on it the whole year. And judging by this stack of cards, Abby has spent twenty times that.

I've let her down. I ignored her and put her off and blew her off and...

I let her down.

I swallow the growing lump in my throat and pick up the cards, flipping through them. They're thick, probably a hundred deep, and neatly numbered. Half are yellow, half pink.

Did she know I would need this? Did she know I wouldn't know the first thing about our presentation?

"Ann, Abby, you're up."

I realize the teacher is staring at me. I nod and pull my hood down and pick up the cards. They're heavy in my hands, evidence of the ways I've disappointed her.

I'm numb with the realization that I deserted her, left her to do all the work. Ignored her as if she meant nothing. Again. Over and over and over.

And instead of seeking revenge and instead of telling the teacher or letting me stand up there mute, she did it all. She saved me even though I don't deserve it.

I make my way to the front of the room, where Abby is setting up poster boards.

Thank you, I mouth to her when she looks up.

She just nods, that same empty look in her eyes. The sympathy, the warmth, the friendship, it's all gone. She simply stares back at me as if I'm nothing.

This is her send-off for me. This is the way she'll wash her hands of me. This is how she can let go of me without feeling guilty for doing it. She knows I'm so wrapped up in Connor that we'll never be best friends like we were before.

I've finally lost her.

This is the end for us.

The realization is so strong my knees almost buckle. When this presentation is over, it'll be official. I have no friends.

I am alone.

May 20

EIGHT MONTHS, TWENTY DAYS

His apartment is silent when I arrive. I stop at the door and think there must be something wrong. It is never silent.

My shoes echo on the laminate in the hallway as I make my way back to his bedroom.

When I push open the door, I'm surprised to see that the drapes are open and light is streaming through. Connor is sitting on the ground holding a guitar, leaning over, concentrating.

"Oh, good, sit down!" He's happy to see me, like he's been waiting all day for my arrival, and it makes my mouth turn up in a smile because I remember when he used to do this all the time. It was like he was counting the seconds until I would arrive and we'd be together again.

I nod and go to the chair.

"Tell me if you recognize this." He has picks on each finger and the sounds of his acoustic guitar fill the room, a familiar melody I can't place.

He looks at me expectantly when he's done, his eyebrows raised.

"Wait…I know it…don't tell me…"

He just plays it again, the notes floating on air. His fingers are quick and graceful as they pluck the melody.

He looks up again. I still can't place it. I'm desperate, my mind racing, but I can't place it.

I see the disappointment on his face as he stares at me. As I come up empty. His blue eyes are filled with it, and I scramble, thinking, trying to find the right song.

"It's *Forever Yours*," he says, before I succeed.

"*Oh!*" I say, too loud. "My favorite song."

"Yes."

I smile at him, try to make him see that I'm pleased with his surprise, but he sets the guitar down. I've spoiled it. I didn't recognize my own favorite song. I took away his moment of glory.

"It took me three hours," he says.

"Play it again. Please? It was beautiful. Now that I know what song it is, it'll be even prettier."

For a second he just strums his hands across the strings like he hasn't heard me, like he won't answer at all.

I'm relieved when he nods and picks up the melody again.

I hate it that every little thing has become so important. I have to try so hard every moment of every day to do and say the right thing, or his mood will turn.

And my day will turn with it.

I'm tired of this high-wire act, this balance where I have to be *on* all the time, where I have to perform whenever the light hits me or risk falling.

As the notes fill the room again I lie back on his bed and stare at the popcorn ceiling. Connor sits just a few feet away from me, but it feels like miles. There is a cavernous hole between us, and I can never seem to fill it.

I know that he spent three hours doing this for me, but it's empty because it's not what I want. I want him to stop making everything so hard. I want him to smile at me and I don't want to see the things in his eyes that tell me it's not real.

I want him to be whole so I don't have to try so hard to make him that way.

I want to not care if I make a mistake. I want this to be easy and happy, and I want to not walk on eggshells every moment of every day. I want to say the wrong thing and see him smile anyway.

I want him to hang out with me and my friends. I want him to come over for dinner with my mom and I want to be able to leave the room and not worry about what they are saying to each other.

The longing is so fierce I feel it in my chest, an ache that makes my whole body weak.

I want to be forgiven for my mistakes. I want them to wash away every day and I want a clean slate. I don't want them to stack up higher and higher, like a house of cards ready to topple with the breeze.

I want him to leave behind everything from his childhood and look only at the future we have together. I want him to focus on his job and his apartment and pretend he doesn't have parents at all, that I'm his family and we can find happiness and success together and nothing can touch him.

I want it to be like I thought it was going to be when we met. Like I thought it was going to be the first time I said those three words and realized I meant them.

But he will never let go of his pain. And that is all I want for him.

August 30
ONE YEAR

I'm rocking back and forth, still sitting on the ground wrapped in a blanket, when I hear it: a car door. The telltale squeak tells me it is Connor's truck. I'd know that sound anywhere.

My heart seems to spasm in my chest, first half-stopping, and then galloping off in a thunderous roar. My chest seems to heave and pulsate with my heartbeats. Nausea wells up.

Connor is back.

I'm not even sure how long he was gone. I lost all sense of time since I landed here, amidst the mess and carnage.

Has it been minutes or hours? Is he back because he's still angry—or has he realized what he's done?

This is so much worse than anything before. He must know that. Does he think he can walk in and apologize and hold me?

Would I let him?

I look up at the door. The chain is still locked. So is the deadbolt, which Connor doesn't have a key to because he lost it. He can't get in, not until I let him in. Not until I am ready.

Unless he does something crazy like break the window. Would he do that? Is he that angry? Or maybe he's worried. Maybe he knows he went too far this time.

I listen to his footsteps approach, and with each step my breathing gets more erratic.

I am afraid of him.

I am truly afraid.

May 18

EIGHT MONTHS, EIGHTEEN DAYS

I can't figure out what set him off.

He broke two dishes while trying to wash them. That was the start. And now he rakes his hands across the wall and knocks all the pictures off, and when I go to pick them up, he turns on me.

"Get out," he says. He spits the words at me. "I'm so sick of looking at you."

I don't know where he expects me to go. If I walk through the front door of my mom's house tonight, she'll take one look at my red eyes and know he caused it again, and that will make things even harder. She'll want to know everything. And I can't explain any of this. Not even if I had all day. No one will understand this.

I crouch on the ground and pick up shards of glass, ignoring the malice in his voice. "Just let me pick this up. You're not even wearing shoes."

But he ignores me and steps into the glass and pushes me over with his leg, and I can't catch my balance before I fall and knock my head into the wall and a flash of pain blinds me.

"I don't want you to see me like this today. Just *get out,*" he says again.

I breathe in and out slowly, stalling for time. "Connor, just go sit down, okay? Just go play your guitar or—"

"Fuck that stupid guitar!"

I swallow and fight the urge to look up at him. His face is so ugly when he's this angry. I don't like to see it. It haunts me, like a ghost that hangs around even when his anger is gone. I can see it behind his eyes, even when he smiles. It reminds me that there will always be more of this, that it will happen again and again and again until I can figure out how to be everything he needs me to be.

I swallow hard and get my feet back under me and stand up, doing it slowly, like I don't know what I'll find once I'm on my feet again.

And he watches me, calculating, and I know he will have something to say when I get to him.

But he surprises me. He doesn't say anything. He just pushes me backward until I'm against the wall and he towers over me. The glass still litters the floor around us.

His face is so close that his nose brushes mine. "Why the fuck do you just sit around like this? Why the fuck do you put yourself in my way?"

I swallow, slowly, waiting. I never speak when he's like this. The words belong to him.

"Are you that fucking stupid? Do you *want* me to hit you?"

My breath comes in shallow, quick bursts through my mouth, because my nose is already stuffed from the tears. I hate this so much. If he's going to do it, I wish he would just do it.

He is so ugly right now. His eyes are empty when he's like this. His anger consumes him, and Connor is gone. He is a product of his childhood.

It is what it is, and I know I have to wait for him to come back to me.

And I know that when the anger is gone, and he's back, he will cry for what he's done to me. He'll mean every word he says, every apology. But it won't stop it from happening again.

I don't know what to do anymore. I think I might actually have to get away from him for anything to get better. I think about it, for tiny little moments, until that pain sears through my chest and I realize I can't do it. I realize I love him too much, and the mere thought of leaving makes my heart throb a dull ache.

The house is so still. So frozen, as he stares at me. Long moments pass and I just keep waiting. Waiting for the moment chaos breaks loose. It will happen. It always happens.

And yet he just stares at me, that ugly look in his eyes, and something inside me snaps and I shove him. Hard. He has no time to react. He just topples over and lands in the glass, and a piece slices his palm.

I'm so stunned by my own actions I don't move. I don't know how I could have done that. I don't know how I just let loose and did that after all these months of just *taking it*. I stand there, eyes wide, and fear snakes its way up me and coils in my stomach and throat.

I should not have done that.

He's up like lightning and he's in my face again. I retreat, but only succeed in smacking my head against the wall yet again. It's pounding now, a steady beat that keeps up with my racing heart.

"You shouldn't have done that," he says, as if he can read my thoughts. His voice is so calm. So even. So murderous. It's worse than the moments he is uncontrollable.

Because he's scheming, calculating his next move.

And then he turns away from me, and it unleashes.

The half-eaten dinner goes first, flying across the room and splattering like red paint on the wall. A dining room chair shoots past me, inches from my head.

His palm is still bleeding from the glass. It drips on the carpet, seeps in. "Why can't you just fucking *hate me*?"

He doesn't expect an answer. He's tearing apart his place. He grabs a remote and hurls it across the room, into a mirror, and it splinters into a web of cracks.

And all I can think is *seven years bad luck*. As if that matters, as if we have any luck at all.

"You're too good for this! You're too good for all of this!"

He picks up a lamp and it flies across the room, the cord trailing after.

And then he's done with it as quickly as he snapped into it. He slides to the ground, silent. There are no tears, no shouts, nothing. He's simply empty.

I walk through the carnage and drop to the ground, then lie down and rest my head in his lap. He doesn't seem to see me. His eyes are vacant. He just strokes my hair with one hand, and I close my eyes and try to disappear.

We are traveling down a path with no happy ending, and it's too late to turn around.

May 14

EIGHT MONTHS, FOURTEEN DAYS

I'm standing in line at the coffee shop in town, waiting on my order, when Abby walks in. Just seeing her makes my stomach hurt. Why can't this be any other day? I wish I'd showered and dressed in something bright and happy, that she'd see me laughing with Connor.

But it's just me. And I'm exhausted after a night of talking Connor down off the edge yet again. I don't even like coffee, but I'm buying it because I need the caffeine to get through finals.

And I have nothing to do but wait here as she walks up, a tentative smile on her face. She stands in front of me, looking at me, for too long.

"How are you?" she finally says.

She knows how I am. She can see it. Does she want me to say it out loud? Does she want me to admit I'm tired and haunted and just *weary* of all this?

"Good," I say.

It's a lie and she knows it, but she just lets it hang there. "That's good."

I want to hug her. I want to leave Starbucks with her and get in her car and go wherever she's going and pretend her life is mine. I could live like her. I know I could. A world where your parents sit at the dinner table and ask you how your day was. A world where they tuck you in at night and you roll your eyes and act annoyed, but you secretly love it.

"My mom wants to know why you're never over anymore."

My coffee is sitting in front of me now. I should just walk away. I don't have to answer her.

"What did you tell her?"

"That you hate me," she says. Her voice is even. Like saying those words is no effort at all.

"I don't hate you." My voice is barely above a whisper as I say it, as I look at her to see if that really is what she thinks. I'm the one who abandoned her, not the other way around. I'm the one who ignored her calls and barely nodded at her in the hallways at school. It was me. She did nothing to deserve hate.

She doesn't answer. She just picks at her nails and we

stand in silence, two old friends with nothing to say to one another.

"And Connor? How's he?"

She knows how he is. She knows *who* he is, and that is enough.

"Fine."

Fine. Everything is fine. She knows this, too, is a lie. I don't know why I insist on saying it.

She starts to leave.

"I mean—"

I don't know what I mean. I don't know why I stopped her.

She turns back to me and looks me in the eye for the first time.

I know she sees who I am now. I know she pities me. The silence hangs between us like a weight, and neither of us has to say anything to know what has gone unspoken.

And then she hugs me. It lasts at least five seconds longer than necessary and I close my eyes and lose myself in it, a hug more secure than anything I've felt in months.

And then without looking at me again, she walks away.

And I know that she's a real friend. And I wish I could have her back again.

May 7

EIGHT MONTHS, SEVEN DAYS

I think I might be pregnant. I don't know how it happened. I don't know what to do or say. All day long, every
time my stomach twinges, I think it might be cramps and
I rush to the bathroom, but it's not.

We were so careful.

I know he cannot handle this. I know I need to find
out first, before I say anything. He has too much on his
plate. He has too much to deal with. I can't add this to it.

All day at school, I've been distracted. I keep counting
the days on my fingers, in my notebooks, but every time,
it's the same. I am two days late.

This can't happen. This will ruin it all. It will be the

straw that breaks the camel's back. Some people can handle things like this. We can't. Not now.

PE is the worst. I was supposed to be playing basketball, but after the third time I got hit with the ball, I feigned sick and left.

It's not a lie. I do feel sick. I don't know if I'm sick because I'm really pregnant or I'm sick because I'm so scared, but either way, I feel weak and vaguely nauseous. I need to lie down. In a dark hole where no one will find me ever again.

I can't have a baby. Not now. Not in this world. Things have to be fixed first. Connor and I have to figure out how to take care of ourselves first. He has to get better at controlling his anger and be happy, and we have so many things to fix.

I leave before sixth period. I don't even care that a guard sees me pull out of the gravel lot, rocks flying behind my little car. I know he wrote down my plate. I know I will get detention for this. It seems silly, detention. Childish. Do they really think I would care?

I drive to Aberdeen, the next town over where no one will recognize me, and find a drug store. I'm ashamed of what I'm doing. I know I'm eighteen. It could be worse. But this is so wrong.

I buy three tests, just to be safe. I don't want to have to come back if one doesn't work right. I don't want to stand at the register, praying the clerk uses a bag you can't see through. I hate every second of it.

My stomach is twisting and turning so hard it's painful.

This can't happen. It will ruin everything. It will ruin me, break Connor, and spite my mother. She'll hate me for sure now.

I take the tests to McDonald's and park in the lot, staring at those stupid golden arches that seem too bright and perky, that seem to be mocking me.

I'm frozen. If I go inside and take this test and it says positive, it will mean so many things. Things I can't handle. It will mean my life is really over. It will mean I can never be the person I used to be. I can never return to who I once was.

And I will have to tell him and I don't think I can do that. I don't think I can put that on his shoulders when they already sink with the weight of the world he carries. I don't think I can look him in the eyes and watch the disappointment and despair I'm sure will be there. A baby doesn't deserve a reaction like that. A reaction like I'm feeling right now—the utter dread and fear. A baby is supposed to be a happy thing, not a death knell.

An hour passes before I finally stuff all three boxes into my purse. If I don't do this now, I never will. I have to know. Not knowing is killing me.

I walk across the tile floor as if it's the plank, and these tests are my scarlet letter for all to see.

The bathroom is empty. I take the big handicap stall and hang my purse on the door. I set a box on the top of the paper dispenser, my hand a little shaky, and then I slide my jeans down and sit down on the toilet.

And then I see it … and then I know.

I'm not pregnant.

The relief I feel is so swift and intense I collapse and bury my face in my arms, and rest on my knees and sob.

All alone, in the McDonald's bathroom.

April 30
EIGHT MONTHS

For two days, I skipped school. Two days I avoided everything. I stayed in bed almost all day, the curtains drawn, the covers pulled up to my chin.

But I know I have to go back to class before I miss too much. Before they call my mom.

I bring a stool into the tiny bathroom in his apartment and sit on it under the harsh light, and stare at the angry blue bruise under my eye.

Gingerly, I touch the darkest spot and wince. It's still tender even though it's been a few days. It's turning a grotesque shade of yellow around the edges.

I dig through a bag of makeup, trying to find the best

concealer. I choose the weird green goop and pat it under my eye, then follow it up with foundation and powder. I just need to cover it up so no one will see it. I'll keep my head down and get through class. The bruise will fade and no one will ever know it was there.

I look up after I dab another layer of powder under my eye.

It's not an improvement. I look like I've spackled pancake batter on my face.

I take a washcloth and wipe it off, but the pressure makes my whole face throb.

I look down at the linoleum for a moment and take a few deep breaths to will away the emotions welling up in my chest. This is stupid. I need to just cover it up and get to school.

I can do this.

I grip the sink and stare straight back at my reflection.

And I don't recognize myself.

Before I can stop it, my lip starts quivering. A tiny bit at first, then it's shaking and I have to bite it. My vision shimmers, and then I see the big tears brim and roll down my cheeks, dripping off my chin, one after another.

The girl staring back at me is not me.

It is someone else.

It is not me.

Her eyes turn red as I watch her in the mirror. Her sparkling blue eyes look so hollow.

She's like the zombie version of me. The undead version.

There is no way that is me.

I close my eyes because I can't look at her anymore.

School can wait. I can make up another day. It's Friday, anyway. By Monday the bruise will be gone and no one will have to know about it.

I need to go back to bed, where the world doesn't exist.

I swipe my hand across the counter and the makeup crashes to the floor, and then I walk out the door and switch off those ugly bright lights.

I'm going back to bed. And when I wake up maybe that ugly girl will be gone.

April 27

SEVEN MONTHS, TWENTY-EIGHT DAYS

I should have known when he said, "You're so lucky I don't hit girls," that one day he would.

And he did. He just hit me. I can't seem to process it. I'm too shocked to move, as the same image replays over and over in my mind. The way his knuckles smashed into my cheek, the loud *crack* when skin met skin.

Connor wouldn't do that to me. He wouldn't turn on me like that. He hits things, not people. He told me that himself, that first month we were together, when I saw all those scars on his knuckles.

He loves me as much as I love him. And he would never hurt me like this.

But I know by the look on his face that he's more stunned than I am, and that it has really, truly happened.

He hit me.

I just keep thinking it, over and over, trying to wrap my head around it. I just keep staring at him, my face stinging so hard it burns. This didn't happen. He doesn't even look angry anymore. It couldn't have happened.

I sink to the ground but he catches me, picks me up before I can slide all the way to the floor. He carries me to the couch and sets me down as if I'm glass, as if I might break.

He doesn't see that I'm already broken.

Tears flow down his cheeks and slide off his jaw. "I'm sorry. I'm so sorry." He keeps repeating it.

He's so far away. I'm so deep inside myself that I can't respond, can't talk.

He's done it. He's hit me.

He touches the spot on my cheek with the backside of his fingers. I'm sure it is red. It is swelling; I can feel it grow, heat spreading across my face. My eye feels heavy, like it's trying to close all on its own.

"Oh, God, Ann, I'm sorry," he keeps saying. Over and over. It is his mantra. He is sorry.

He's kissing my face and my hands and crying.

"I swear to you I didn't mean to. I don't know why I did that. I'm so sorry. So, so sorry."

I know he is. I know he hadn't wanted to do that.

Just like I knew he would. It was inside him. I know that. I knew that it would come out.

And even though I thought I was ready, I wasn't.

What do you do when the one person you want comfort from the most is the one who caused your pain? How can I want so desperately for him to wrap me up in his arms but also want so much for him to leave me alone?

"Please," I whisper, though I have nothing else to say. "Please."

I don't know what I'm asking of him. I don't know what I want right now, except to rewind the last ten minutes and erase it all.

It didn't happen.

No.

It didn't happen.

He is sobbing. I can't make out his words anymore because they garble together into incoherent babble between his tears.

Hitting me has broken him. What his father failed to do, he has done himself.

All the times he has cried for himself, cried for the things he'd lived through, he's never sobbed like this.

But now he knows. Now he knows, just as I have known on some level, what is inside him. It lurks behind his eyes, growing and changing and waiting.

And now it has happened. Now we both know who he is.

We both know *what* he is.

He cannot deny it anymore.

And neither can I.

April 25

SEVEN MONTHS, TWENTY-SIX DAYS

Connor is in the kind of mood I rarely see him in. The kind where he smiles and cracks jokes. The kind that give me hope that someday he'll be whole again. I know if we can make a life for ourselves, away from all the drama of his old life, he could be like this all the time.

People don't understand us. They don't understand me. They think it's so black and white, that he makes me miserable and that I should be with someone else and that I deserve something else.

But it's not black and white at all. It's gray. It's a never-ending world of gray.

They don't understand that there is so much to him

that they'll never see. That he only shows to me. They don't understand that late at night, he tells me how beautiful I am. He tells me all the things he will give me one day, when our problems are over. They don't understand that he would die for me.

We are going sailing today. After last week, when he missed our appointment, he used his own money to rent the boat again. Even though I know he can't afford it. Even though I know it means he isn't going to pay the light bill so that we can do this.

I don't care, because this moment is all I need to get through the darkness.

He's holding my hand and talking about sleeping on the boat. He wants to tie it to a buoy out in the bay and stay there overnight, listening to the water and forgetting about everything but the moment and the night.

I think it's the best thing I've ever heard.

Connor knows exactly what to do and he shows me how to untie the boat from the dock and flip the bumpers over the edge of the little railing. He motors out of the marina and then I hold on to the little rudder and he starts tugging on nylon lines and whipping things around and in seconds the boat picks up speed and we are gliding, and he kills the engine.

The silence is beautiful. All I hear is the water and the way it splashes the bow, and the sound of the sail as it slaps around if he turns the boat out of the wind.   .

He's concentrating, so I lean back on the bench and let the sun warm my face, and I relax. For the first time in weeks, I let the tension leave my body and let myself dream of life like this, when Connor is always happy and things are just... easy.

We sail for nearly an hour before Connor speaks.

"You look cute on this boat. It suits you."

I open my eyes and look at him, still in my dreamlike state. "You look cute sailing."

He grins at me, one of his genuine smiles. "I love you," he says.

"I know. I love you too."

He tilts his head and stares at me, his blue eyes sparkling with such genuine happiness it brings tears to my eyes, happy tears for once, and I have to slide over and get closer to him. He keeps one hand on the rudder and wraps his free one around me. The wind is whipping my hair around, making it dance, and it gets in his face but he doesn't move away from me.

"I'm so glad I found you. You're everything to me. I couldn't do this without you. I would have given up a long time ago."

I know that he doesn't mean it figuratively; I know it's literal. I know there were nights he wanted to find a bridge and jump right off. But he knew I would be there for him. He knew that together, we could do anything, and life could be good for him. For us.

I try to get closer to him, though it's not possible.

"I wish we could do this every single day," he says. "I wish this was our life."

I nod. "It will be, some day. We'll get a boat and we'll

fill it with food and fishing poles and we'll sail the world. And we won't give anyone our phone number or anything, and no one will be able to touch us."

He sighs and rests his lips against my temple, and I close my eyes. There are no shooting stars or wishbones or magic dust, but I make a wish anyway.

I wish that we both last long enough for it to happen.

April 18

SEVEN MONTHS, NINETEEN DAYS

We were supposed to go sailing today. We were supposed to be alone together and have a day on the water and forget about the problems that plague us.

But he's not here. I sit on the dock next to our rented sailboat, listening to the seagulls and the lapping water, and I wait.

And wait.

But he doesn't show and I do not know why. I try to imagine what he could be doing, what dragged him away from something he was so excited about.

But it doesn't matter, because even when he explains why, I will not understand. I will never know why he does the things he does because I have never lived his life. Because he has lived things I can't even dream.

I'm glad no one can see me right now. I think they might see my hopes dashed, like they are real things dancing on the water and someone might see them drown, just like that, gone forever. And then they would pity me, and I don't want that. I don't need that. I choose the things that happen in my life and I don't need anyone feeling sorry for me.

I lie back on the dock and listen to the sounds and give up on the idea of seeing him.

It doesn't matter. It wouldn't have lived up to my hopes anyway.

April 1

SEVEN MONTHS, TWO DAYS

Today is his birthday, just two weeks after my own. He's nineteen.

His father has been gone for four days. We both hope he stays away. Everything takes on such a beautiful peace when he's gone. The tension leaves Connor's body. He doesn't have to float around, constantly watching out for his mom. He can be himself.

It's just like those first few weeks after I met him, when Jack and Nancy were on one of their breaks. I hope it lasts longer this time. I hope it lasts forever.

Connor is at work. The job is too new for him to take his birthday off, even though I know he wanted to.

I'm baking a cake with his mom, her first time hanging out at his apartment. She seems happier today. The wrinkles seem lighter. Her hair doesn't look so gray.

Finally, I know what it is to live in a world without Jack. And I wish he would just fade away and disappear. None of us would miss him.

It feels weird to hang out with his mom. She likes me, I know that. She knows I am there for Connor in a way she never could be, because I'm not forced to choose between him and Jack. She's too busy bending over backward for Jack, too busy walking that razor-thin line of keeping Jack happy.

Connor has always been alone. Even though she loves him, she could never protect him. Not when Connor has to work so hard to protect *her*. Connor doesn't judge her for it, but I think I do. I want to ask her, I want to know why she would keep Connor around someone like Jack, especially when he was little and helpless. I want to ask her why she couldn't just divorce him.

Why she ruined Connor's life by not just leaving Jack and finding somewhere else to be, some*one* else to be. I wonder who Connor would be if she had done that. I wonder if life would be as easy as I imagine it could be if he weren't so scarred by it all.

She's assembling a big dish of tamales, his favorite, and I'm frosting the cake. There is country music playing on the beat-up stereo mounted under the kitchen cabinets.

I feel as if there are so many things she wants to say to

me. I think I can actually see her words hanging around us, like a big cloud, and I wait for them to rain down.

It feels weird. Uncomfortable but not. With my mom, there's judgment. I know she just wants what's best for me, but I hate that she thinks she knows what I need more than I know. She can't just say her opinion once. It's this nonstop battle with her, and she won't give up until I leave him.

And all it does is ensure that I avoid her. It's making things so much worse. And I wish she'd just see it and stop bringing him up all the time. Why can't she ask me about anything but him?

But not with Nancy. With Nancy, there's just quiet.

Connor gets home from work just as dinner is finished. He's covered in sawdust but he smiles at us and gives me a kiss on his way to the shower. "Be out in twenty."

But she doesn't last that long. Jack calls and she is gone, saying nothing to me as she glances back just before the door shuts. When Connor leaves the bathroom he sees only me.

And he doesn't have to ask to know. He grabs a plate and smiles at me, but it's not the same smile as twenty minutes ago.

We each dish up too many tamales, more than we can eat, so the pan won't be filled with the ones Nancy would have eaten. And then we sit across from each other at the table, but the only sounds are our forks and knives.

"I baked you a cake," I say.

"Thanks," he says, between bites.

I wish she was still here. I wish she hadn't ruined it. I wish, for one night, she had picked Connor over Jack.

But I know the repercussions of doing that and I know why she didn't.

When we're both full, I scrape our dishes into the trash. We didn't eat it all. There is too much left. The pan sits on the stove like a neon sign.

Connor joins me in the living room, on the couch he bought at the Salvation Army. He has no TV yet.

I pull a small wrapped gift from under the couch and hand it to him.

"You didn't have to."

"Yes I did. Open it."

The box is tiny, wrapped with silver paper and invisible tape I'd carefully chosen. He rips it off and slides off the lid. A slip of paper is all the box contains, and he looks up at me, confused.

"It's a reservation. We're going sailing."

His eyes light up. I've done well.

"Oh, babe, thank you." He wraps his arms around me and I close my eyes, reveling in this moment.

His dad had a sailboat when he was a kid. It only lasted a year, but Connor was hooked. He talks about it constantly.

I can't wait for it. A whole day, just me and him and the water. I hope that on that day, we will have peace. Just for a day, away from everything.

I wonder what would happen if we could just sail away and never come back.

March 19

SIX MONTHS, NINETEEN DAYS

I'm in my room when she comes home. I had hoped I wouldn't see her today.

It's my birthday. I'm eighteen, and today I plan to leave and never come back.

I'm not going far. Just to Connor's apartment across town. It's his, not mine, but I will stay there. I just feel like an unwanted house guest here.

I'm tired of my mom. I'm tired of the fights. Every time she sees me, she brings him up. He is all I am to her, and until he is gone, I am no one. She uses every second she can to poke at him, pick at our relationship, to find the cracks and exploit them.

If she thinks that's going to make me choose her over him, she's wrong.

I'm tired of having to defend him to her. She doesn't understand that he's going to be someone. She doesn't get that he may seem like a bad person on the outside, he may be aloof or cold, but if you give him a chance, he's so much more.

Even though all his life people have put him down, he wants so much to get out of it. He got his GED when he was sixteen, after his dad made it hard to get to school every day. He started working right away, saving for the day he could move out and get his own place. He'll triumph even after all his dad has done to keep him down. These are the things I see in him. The way he makes lemonade out of lemons.

It's not his fault his life is one big lemon. All he needs is for people to give him a chance. I think one day, when we have some money saved up, we will move away and get a place far from home. And we will start over, and he will leave everything behind and forget everyone who doubts him.

Together we will find happiness again. We will take back everything that was robbed from him.

From me.

My mom proved exactly what he said: that people see him and judge him and don't give him a chance.

My stomach sinks when I hear the gentle hum of the garage door. I knew I should have left the rest of this stuff.

I knew it. I could have gone back to Connor's and forgotten all about it, and avoided seeing her.

I could have written her a note, explaining it all. Maybe I could have said something nice, because I would have done it alone, not in the heat of the moment. Maybe it would have helped us.

But I know now we'll have to talk, and the words will run away from us and we'll both say too much.

Her footsteps creak on the stairway. I freeze. My door is open and she will see me on the way to her room. It's too late to hide.

I just keep stuffing things in the duffle bag like I don't care if she sees me. Like it won't shock her to realize I'm leaving.

It's not like she planned anything for my eighteenth birthday anyway. I'm not that girl anymore. The one who has cake and burgers and opens presents at the dining room table. She knows it, just like I know it. There's no reason to pretend anymore.

She passes the door before stopping. I know she's just three feet down the hall, but she doesn't make a sound.

Several long seconds tick by as I keep shoving stuff into the bottom of the bag. Why isn't she speaking? Why hasn't she come back?

And then she does. She stands in the doorway, filling it as she leans against one side of the jamb and crosses her arms. Her hair is lighter than it was last I saw her. But the bags under her eyes are bigger, thicker, puffier. She looks haunted.

"Don't," she says, so quietly I'm not sure I heard it at all.

It's the only word she says. I just stare back at her, and then stuff a hooded sweatshirt into the bag. I'm afraid if I say anything, it'll all come out. All the bitterness of all the years between us without a single *I love you*. The thought of all those wasted years, waiting for her to act like she used to, waiting for her to hug me and tuck me in at night, stabs into me like a jagged knife, and I try hard not to dwell on it. I try hard to pretend I don't care, just like she does.

Except I don't think she's pretending anymore. Maybe before Connor came along we could have fixed it. Back then there weren't a bunch of harsh words between us. There were just three unspoken ones. I bet I could have gotten them out of her. I bet she would have meant them, too.

But not now. Now everything's ruined. I might as well just be with him all the time, because I'm pretty sure she hates me now. I'm pretty sure she thinks I hate her, too.

I don't, though. I love her so much it hurts. Something deep inside aches to drop the bags and rush to her and wrap my arms around her and wait for her to do the same to me, even though she never would. She's the ice queen, and she'll never thaw. And that's why I have to get out of here.

I walk up to her and we stand like that, neither of us looking at each other. I just look at the strap on my duffel bag as I twist it around in my hands.

"He's not good enough for you," she says.

"You don't know him."

"Why do you have to be with him? I know you want to help him. Why can't you do that as friends?"

"I don't want to be just friends with him. I love him," I say, anger edging into my voice. I knew she would do this. This is why I didn't want to see her. This is why I avoid her. She takes my one piece of happiness and twists it into something ugly.

"You think you love him. You're seventeen." She uncrosses and recrosses her arms, like she's trying to look angry and serious and in charge, but I don't care.

"Eighteen," I say. My anger is boiling now. I hate that she does this. Every single time I see her, she does this. I don't want to be in the same room with her anymore if all we're going to do is have the same argument over and over again. There are no winners, only losers, and I'm tired of being one of them.

"You wanted to go to college, Ann." She pushes away from the door jamb to stand at her full height, staring straight at me and daring me to disagree.

"College has nothing to do with him!"

She takes a step into the room, her sensible little pumps sinking into the carpet. "It's not just a coincidence. It's about him. You've had college plans for years, and then six months with him and it changes. You don't know *what* you want anymore."

"Yes, I do! And I want to be with him. Not here. Not

with you. All you ever do is put him down. You're just like his dad."

I want to leave, right now, before I break my teeth from clenching them so hard. But I won't touch her, and she's in my way. I sling the duffel over my shoulder and walk up to her, staring at the space between her eyes instead of looking her *in* the eyes.

"He's the reason you've given everything up. He's not worth it."

"Don't, Mom," I say, desperate for her to stop before I snap. "Please, just *shut up*."

The words bite. I see it in her face. But I have to stop her.

"Please, just don't," I say, quieter this time.

She steps aside and I rush past before I can apologize. Before I can break down.

I hate that our relationship has boiled down to Connor and nothing else. I don't know why she can't see past him to be there for me.

I want this to end. I want it all over. I want her to rush after me and tell me she loves me and just wants what's best for me, and that she won't judge me if I think that's something different than she does.

But she never will. I see that now.

And that is why I'm leaving.

March 14

SIX MONTHS, FOURTEEN DAYS

I've been working on the sculpture for six hours. It's a little over half complete—half a heart. It sort of looks like some kind of weird bowl, hollow in the middle. I could probably fill it with chips if I wanted to.

But I don't have any chips, or soda, or anything. I've been working since nine o'clock this morning without stopping.

It looks beautiful, too. The glow of the lamp casts a mosaic splash of color across the table. I just wish it was further along. It's been hard to get the exact right amount of glue. Too little and it doesn't hold. Too much and it ruins the effect of the glass.

It has to be perfect. Each piece has to fit together like a puzzle. Like it went together all along, not like it's a thousand broken pieces.

I'm getting a headache from the glue fumes, so I decide to take a break and go get some lunch. Maybe a little fuel and some caffeine will perk me up enough that I can work for another hour or two.

I leave the house and jump in my car, holding the wheel with two fingers because it's cold to the touch.

I wind down the hills, the view of the ocean disappearing as I descend to sea level. I park near the front door of the grocery store and go inside, swinging my keys around one finger.

I'm in the candy aisle, debating between Mike and Ike and Good & Plenty when Abby walks up to me. She's wearing cute bootcut jeans with electric blue heels and a hoodie with a big smiley face on the front. She used to hate jeans. She only wore skirts.

I wonder when that changed.

"Hey. Are you here with Blake or something?" She stops in front of me, shoving her hands into the pocket on the front of her hoodie. Is she blinking a lot or is it just me? When was the last time we even talked?

I freeze, my hand on the Mike and Ike. "Blake?"

She nods, her eyes narrowing slightly as she studies me. "Yeah. He has a cart filled with junk food. I thought maybe you two—"

"He's here?"

Abby nods. "Yes. Cart. Junk Food. Are you following?"

I nod, debating whether I should just ditch the candy and dash out the door before Blake finds me.

I haven't seen him since that day at the park.

If he finds me now, I know there will be questions. Lots and lots of questions. And Abby is here. God—the two of them together, they'll really lay into me.

I don't need the fifth degree. I just want some snacks and I want to go back home and work on the sculpture.

"Um, no, we're not here together. Actually, I just remembered something—" I start to turn away from her, but she grabs me by the arm.

"Don't lie." Her voice is quiet, soft, pleading. "Please, just don't lie. I get why you blow me off. I get why things have changed. But you've never lied to me. Just don't start now, okay?"

I nod, slowly, staring down at her fingers and her French-manicured nails. She releases my arm and I look up at her.

I don't know how she manages to be so understanding. I don't think I could do that, if the roles were reversed. If my best friend ditched me for a boy. But she gets it. Somehow, she gets it.

"Thank you. For … for just being you."

She nods solemnly and takes a step back. "I'll go talk to him. Go pay for your stuff."

I nod back at her, but I'm frozen, just staring at her nose, a thousand feelings and thoughts swirling until I'm lost to them, and she grabs my shoulder and gives it a small shake. "Hey. If you don't want to talk to him, then go. Okay?" She sighs and releases my shoulder. "And Ann?"

I look up at her.

"If you ever need me or want to talk, or..."

I nod.

"Good."

I just nod again and grab the Mike and Ike and scurry out of the aisle, not looking back.

Abby is a goddess.

And I'm just...

I don't know what I am anymore.

But I'm not who I used to be.

March 12

SIX MONTHS, TWELVE DAYS

I was kicked off the track team today. Too many missed practices, he said. Said I wasn't dedicated to it anymore.

I know I should care. I know it should hurt. This was my senior year. I was going to rule the place. I was going to beat my record for long jump and win my first two-mile.

But even as the words left the coach's mouth, I was over it. Things like track and high school aren't as important to me as they once were. The hours I spent with the team every day, I only thought of him. I thought of lying next to him on the bed and watching movies. I thought of talking to him and walking with him and being with him.

Sometimes I think I'd give up everything if I could just

spend every day with him, alone in his room, listening to music and just... being together.

I've been running my fastest times all month. Because I knew the second I was done, I would walk to the locker room without even cooling off. I'd still be sweating when I switched into my street clothes. My face would still be flushed when I climbed into my car and left the school in my rearview mirror, heading straight to his place.

Now I have another hour every day for him. Now I can go straight to his house after school and cook us both dinner and wait for him.

I'll have more time to work on my glass sculpture, too. It's taking so much longer than I thought it would. Hours and hours. But I enjoy it. It's become my outlet. When I'm working on it, I think of nothing else. I lose myself in the glass pieces, in the way the light glints off the curved surfaces.

Whenever I have more than a few hours free, I go to the shore and refill my supplies of glass. I find treasures in the sand, reds and greens and blues, and I take them back and imagine where they will go.

The heart will be beautiful when I am done with it. I know it.

I empty my gym locker after I leave the coach's office. I try not to look at the things I stuff into a plastic bag. The shoes and the warm-ups and the meet schedule and the little unopened bag of goldfish crackers I use on away meets.

The pictures inside the door are the hardest, because

even though I don't look at them, it's like the eyes are staring at me.

There were three of us who ran the two-mile. Three of us that were any good at it, anyway. We called ourselves the tripod. Said we could hold up the whole team on our legs, that we would accumulate enough points to keep our school in the lead for divisions.

And we would have. Meets were just about ready to start up for the season. I know we could have done it.

I don't want these pictures anymore. I don't even want them in my bag. I just rip them off the door and let them flutter to the ground and leave them sitting there on the cement floors, under the benches and next to the drains and everywhere. There are so many of them, so many moments frozen like that.

Moments that don't exist anymore. I have no use for moments like that. Superficial moments mean nothing when you know there are so many serious things to think about.

They are still there when I push the door open and step outside, into the light, and walk to my car. It's so early that I know Connor will be at work for another hour.

I have time. For myself. I have not had this in a long time.

I drive to a park two blocks from his apartment and find a picnic table. I pull myself up onto the table and lie back, staring at the blue sky and fluffy white clouds, and I swing my feet back and forth.

The clouds look like bunnies and cotton candy and ridiculous, fluffy, happy things, and they remind me that summer is coming. I'm still wearing sneakers and my warm-ups, but I'm not cold. The air smells like grass. It makes me want an ice cream cone and my old bicycle. I want to go back to that. Back to when Dad was around and life was simple.

I keep swinging my legs, back and forth, and stare at the sky. Moments like this, moments of peace, are rare these days, and I'm enjoying it.

Footsteps break my reverie and I sit up.

Blake. It's hard to suppress the surge of joy I feel at the sight of him.

"Hey," he says.

"Oh. Hi."

He sits down on the bench next to me, so I roll off the table and sit opposite him. His dark hair is messy and all over his forehead, but his eyes are sparkling like he's happy.

Genuine happiness. I hardly recognize it.

"What's up?" I ask, after a long silence. We haven't talked for so long.

"I was going to ask you the same thing."

"I got kicked off track."

Why did I tell him that?

"Why?"

I shrug. "I don't know. Don't care."

"Yes you do. You love track." He tilts his head to the side and leans in, waiting for an answer that will make him understand.

"Did," I say. "Past tense."

"So what do you love now?"

"Connor," I say, without thinking. I want to rewind and keep my mouth shut, but it's out there now.

"And?"

"And that's it." I don't look at him or the sky anymore. I'm staring at the ground—patchy green grass beneath my scuffed white sneakers.

He takes in a long, slow breath. He seems to be filtering through his words, looking for the right ones to say. "Why are you so … different?"

I open my mouth to argue, to say I'm the same Ann I've always been, but I don't. He knows me better than that. And he knows he's right.

"I just am," I say finally. "Please don't start in on me. Everyone is always giving me crap. I don't need it."

"Okay. But listen to me. I'm here if you need me. Ever. Just call. For any reason. I don't care what it is. I don't care what time it is. You can always call me."

I laugh, a sound that comes out too bitter. "Don't be so dramatic."

He grabs my hand and I go still. He stares straight at me, his dark eyes intense. I want to look away and also stare at him forever.

For one long, lingering moment, I see a different future. I see a different me.

But then reality comes back.

"I'm serious," he says.

I wipe the plastic smile off my face and pull my hand away. "I know." I rest my head on the picnic table and close my eyes. "I know."

It seems like I stay like that for an hour. I think he left a long time ago. But when I open my eyes, he's still there.

"What time is it?"

I grab my bag. My keys are not inside. Where are they? They're not in my pocket. Did I lock them in the car? I drop to my knees and look under the table. They have to be here somewhere.

"It's four fifteen."

Four fifteen. God, he got off at four. He could drive by. Right now. He could see me with Blake and get the wrong impression. He's stressed about his job...I don't need to add to it.

"Why are you still here?" I ask.

Blake's face twists. He doesn't understand what's going on. "You just—"

"Go! God, just leave, what's wrong with you?" It comes out so much louder, so much *sharper* than I'd meant it to.

But Connor can't see him. He'll draw conclusions that aren't real. He'll get angry, upset, a lot of things that I don't want to have to deal with today.

"Ann, calm down, what's wrong—"

"Nothing! Just leave, geez!"

I can't find my keys. I dig through my bag but everything falls out. A hairbrush, some change, a pen.

"Here, let me help—"

"Leave!"

I don't even know who I am right now. I'm being a total bitch to him. It's not me. He knows it's not me. Blake steps forward, tries to hug me and calm me down, but I reel back and spin around, and then I see him.

Standing at the edge of the park.

Watching.

He's silent and still, and I realize he's been there awhile.

Before I can breathe, he's crossing the lawn, straight at us, and for one heart-stopping moment I think he will hit Blake. Blake is going to hate me forever and he's going to know the truth about Connor.

But he doesn't. He steps between Blake and me. And then he says in a dangerous voice, "Stay away from her." He spits the words with such malice I want to shrink away, but then he grabs my arm and pulls me, and we are at his truck in seconds. My feet can hardly keep up with his but he's almost holding me off the ground, so it's like I float over there without trying.

My keys are in my pocket now. They were there all along.

"But my car—"

"Leave it," he says.

He's boiling. Simmering, and the lid is going to pop. He's breathing so hard I can hear it. I slide into his truck and barely have the door shut before the tires squeal and we are gone. My head snaps back and I hit it against the sliding window behind my seat.

I know Blake is still standing there at the picnic table. Watching us. And I know he knows what is happening.

And I wish he didn't.

———

Even though Connor moved into his apartment several

weeks ago, there are still boxes everywhere. He doesn't have enough furniture or shelves to unpack things, so they lie around, scattered on the floor.

He comes unleashed when the door is shut.

"Are you cheating on me?

His words steal the breath from my lungs. It's like he shoved me underwater.

I would never cheat on him. I can't believe he'd think I would. "No! God, don't be stupid, I—"

I stop talking and take in a ragged breath of air. That is the one word I know not to say. The one word that is strictly off limits because of how many times his father has said it.

He comes at me so quickly I take an involuntary step backward. My feet get tangled in the boxes and I fall, landing with a hard thud on the thin, shabby carpet. Something is smashed beneath me. I sit awkwardly on top of it, leaning backward on my elbows.

He stops and stands over me. "Don't you *ever* call me stupid. I am not stupid."

I know he's not. I hadn't meant he was stupid. I would never think that about him.

I'm trembling on the floor, surrounded by his things. He doesn't know what he's saying. He's just hurt. He thinks I'm cheating on him. As soon as he knows it's not true, as soon as he knows Blake is only a friend, he'll change. He'll understand. "Please, just listen."

"No. You listen. I won't have you making a fool of me

behind my back. I knew I couldn't trust you. I knew you'd do this!"

"But I didn't do anything!"

"You're lying."

"I'm not. Please calm down, Connor. There's nothing going on."

But he's not himself. He's twisted inside and he's not going to listen to me.

"I knew you would do this! I knew you would find something better and leave me!"

"What are you talking about? I didn't leave! I love you!"

"You're lying! You don't love me! You never have!"

I get up from the floor and stand in front of him. It takes everything I have to stand and look him squarely in the face and not flinch at the way his chest is heaving and the way he stares down at me with such malice I think I see his father in him. It exists in pieces inside him, and it comes out through his eyes.

"Who are you right now? I don't even know you," I say.

He leans in closer, and the words he speaks are carefully chosen, perfectly articulated. "*Fuck you.*"

The silence roars into my ears like a freight train, drowning out the two words he so easily threw out. I think the room may be spinning, but all I can do is stare at his lips and wonder how those words could leave them. Wonder how he could speak them to me. Wonder how I could ever kiss those same lips.

"Please. Just calm down, okay?"

"Calm down? You want me to fucking calm down?" He kicks one of the boxes nearest to me and I hear glass shatter inside. I want to know what it is. I want to know if it's that pretty framed picture of us or that little glass kitten he bought me on our third date.

"Look, I'm just going to go on a walk or something, okay? And you can calm down and then we'll talk about this—" I reach for the door and swing it toward me, but he steps in and slams it shut so hard the walls rattle.

"I'm not done with you!" His voice comes out in a thunderous roar, so loud I recoil. My jaw drops as I stare at him, tears welling in my eyes. Who *is* he? What is he doing? I knew it would upset him to see me with Blake, but...he's never been this...*mean* to me. I mean sure, he has an anger problem...but he promised...he swore it would never be me on the other end of it.

He turns and punches the wall, and big round holes appear in that perfect, freshly painted drywall.

I can't believe he promised me, once, that he would never turn on me like this. I can't believe I trusted that.

I'm so horrified I can't stand anymore. I sink to the floor and land on my knees. I curl over until my face is buried in the carpet. It smells like shampoo.

And then I cry. The tears tumble out so quickly they come like rain, and I can't stop them. He goes silent when he hears the sobs.

I don't know what he's doing and I don't look at him. But he stands there as I sob.

And then he's beside me, and his arm is around me.

The arm that had been so taut, so ready to throw punches, is now gathering me to him in a hug that is not reciprocated.

"I'm sorry, I don't know what I'm doing. I'm sorry."

I just cry harder. I don't like him when he's like this.

I love him so much.

But sometimes I don't like him.

August 30
ONE YEAR

As his footsteps ascend the stairs—getting louder with each passing moment—I find myself scooting back until I'm pushed up against the bed with nowhere else to go.

I listen as he tries the door. It doesn't budge.

He takes his keys out of his pocket. I can hear them shaking and jingling as he slides them into the lock, even over the rain pounding on the roof.

I lean back against the bed frame, waiting. Does he know I'm still here? Maybe he will think I locked up and left.

And yet another part of me is desperate for the door to open, for him to rush to me and gather me in his arms and make this pain disappear. I need him. I want to bury my face in his chest and cry and let him wipe away my tears.

He gets the knob unlocked, and I can see it turning, but the door doesn't move. He stops trying and stands there in silence. He must realize I've locked the deadbolt.

"Ann?"

With one word, I can determine his mood. The anger is gone, melted away as fast as it arrived.

"Sweetheart?" he says, his voice tentative.

He doesn't deserve to call me sweetheart. The fact that he would makes anger mix with the bitter sadness that keeps choking in my throat.

"Honey, I know you're in there. You car is still here."

Damn.

"Ann, I'm sorry. I don't know what I was doing." His voice is shaky, childlike. He knows he went too far. He was so big an hour ago and now he sounds so small.

I pull my knees up to my chest and rest my forehead on them and start humming to myself.

I can't get up and open the door.

I *can't*.

So why do I want to so badly? How can I be that girl, over and over?

I'm not his equal anymore. I'm his doormat; his punching bag.

It happened in pieces, tiny little turning points. I'll never figure out when it all turned, because it wasn't a single moment.

It doesn't matter how many times I look back, how

many times I try to figure it out. There is no before and after. Just a year of choices.

And now I'm here, sitting on the floor, afraid to open the door to the person I love most.

Maybe if I ignore him long enough, he'll leave, and I won't have to choose.

Maybe I'll just stay here for eternity.

March 10

SIX MONTHS, TEN DAYS

It's late, but neither of us can sleep.

And so we're lying in bed, side by side, our fingers intertwined. It's cold in his new apartment, but neither of us are willing to slide from the warmth of the down comforter to turn on the heat, so we just burrow closer and tuck the blankets around us. The tip of the quilt is just short of my nose.

"Someday I'll have so much money I'll just leave the heat on all night, and you can climb out anytime you want and it'll be warm," he says.

I grin. "And will you do that in-floor heating thing? Where it makes the hardwoods warm on my bare feet?"

"Yep. And I'll buy you a big house, so big you can go to the other side if I'm getting on your nerves."

I push him playfully with my shoulder. I know he's joking. He's never on my nerves.

"And what about vacations? I want to go to Europe."

"Of course. We'll spend three months there and see every country. We'll go up the Eiffel Tower and drift on the canals in Venice. You won't want to come back."

I smile at the image. Someday that's really how life will be. We'll conquer all this stuff together, and we'll both forget about this tumultuous time.

It will be perfect.

"What do you love about me?" I ask. Tonight I want to hear it. I'll savor this memory, hold it close to me, during all those other times when things are rocky.

"Everything," he says, turning to me. He kisses me on the nose. "Your smile. Do you know how rare it is to smile as much as you do? I'm not used to it. And your laugh. And the way you talk. You use your tongue a lot, you know. More than normal."

I laugh and push against him again with my shoulder, a playful nudge.

"And you're smart. I mean, you're going to go to college, right? I've never even planned on something like that, and you just know you'll do it."

I open my mouth to tell him that's not true, but I snap it shut again.

I forgot all the application deadlines, and I haven't told him yet. No, that's a lie. I didn't forget, per se. I was just too wrapped up in him to think about going away. Why bother applying when I couldn't even stand the thought of leaving him behind? I just figured I'd go to community college for a couple of years, then he could go with me when I moved to the university and we'd get an apartment instead of living in a dorm.

These days, even community college seems like too much. I don't want to think about it.

So I don't. Think about it, that is. I just put it out of my mind. I'd rather focus on what's in front of me: an intense, beautiful love. The thing I want more than anything. More than college.

I don't tell him any of this. It would ruin the moment.

"And the way you see people. People like me. You're not judgmental like so many others. You see the good in people and give them a chance. You believe in them. I think I like that the best."

I squeeze his hand. Sometimes, he can make me melt.

"Do me," he says.

I grin and give him a wicked look.

"Not like that," he says. "I mean, tell me what you love."

"I know. I just thought something else might be more fun."

He laughs. I love it when he laughs.

"Okay, for real? I love that you're such a strong person. After everything, you're still here to tell about it and try to be a better person. I love how protective you are of the people you love. You'd do anything for them. I love how you always go after what you want. Whether it's skate-boarding or basketball ... or *me.* "

He moves his arm and wraps it around his shoulders, and I turn toward him so my stomach is alongside his hips, and I sling my leg over him and rest my head on his chest until the warmth of his body seeps into mine.

This is what love is. And I don't think I can ever let it go.

March 8

SIX MONTHS, EIGHT DAYS

Connor is driving like an absolute lunatic. The way he snapped like this, the way he went from happy to absolutely crazy, is scaring me.

I skipped track practice today. Connor seemed to be in one of his moods, and he wanted to spend some time together. I know it makes him feel better to have me around. It's both a blessing and a burden, sometimes, to be needed like that.

When his mom called, we'd been sitting down by the river throwing rocks. She was crying. Something was happening and he couldn't get it out of her, and now here we are racing down these back roads trying to get to her, trying to see what he's done this time.

My heart is beating so hard I think it might jump right out of my chest, and I can't stop this sick feeling weighing down the pit of my stomach. I don't know if it's his driving or my worry, but I'm on the verge of puking. My fingers ache with how hard I'm gripping the door. Connor rounds the last corner by his house so fast the tires squeal and slide, and then he skids to a stop.

The door is open, the screen flapping in the breeze. It's not really spring yet. Too cold for the door to be open like that. He's out of the truck before I can even get my seat belt undone. It's jammed.

I struggle with it for a moment, wanting to scream the whole time, not knowing what's happening inside, but finally it clicks free and I jump from the truck and sprint across the lawn. When I walk into the house, it's dark and I have to stand at the door and let my eyes adjust.

A hurricane has gone through here. There's nothing on the walls, nothing on the mantle, nothing anywhere but the floor. It's all in pieces and shards all over.

And so is Nancy. She's sitting on the floor sobbing, and Connor is next to her, pulling her to her feet.

She's clutching her arm.

"I don't know what I did...I don't know what I did..." She just keeps repeating it and Connor just keeps saying, "I know, it's okay," and I just keep standing here, wide-eyed, staring.

Their words echo in my ears and yet I feel so far away,

like I'm watching a scene on the television and not standing right in the middle of it.

"Can you get the truck door open? We need to take her to the doctor's."

Connor's voice, so calm and in control, breaks me out of my haze. I nod and spring into action, happy to be doing something, anything. I swing the door open before they're even out the front door, and I hold it as Connor so carefully helps his mother into the truck, and as she moans when she bumps her arm.

I slide in next to her, so she's in the middle, and try not to look at her black puffy eye as it grows shut. Instead, I just stare straight ahead.

Connor drives much more carefully to the clinic, as if his mother might finally break altogether if he rounds a corner too quickly or hits a speed bump at more than three miles per hour. It's tortuous, sitting here next to her. She's so silent now. She just holds her wrist and stares at nothing.

Eventually we arrive and Connor helps his mom out and I just stand there, next to the truck, as they walk away. I don't want to go in and I don't think Connor has even noticed, because he's concentrating on his mom, on her slow, ginger steps. She's walking like she's eighty.

But then he glances back at me, my hand still on the door, and he smiles just the slightest bit and mouths, "Thank you," as he looks at me.

And I just nod and climb back into the truck, where I wait for the next two hours.

Connor and I scoop the remains of Nancy's things into a big plastic bag. She's in her room, knocked out thanks to the concoction of pain killers prescribed to her.

I wish I could glue all this back together. I wish I could make it good as new again. But I can't, so I just shovel more of it into the bags. Connor takes a full sack out to the curb and then comes back and collapses on the couch and stares at the ceiling, and I can see that he's drained.

"How many times has this happened?" I ask as I put a little angel figurine, missing its wings, into the bag.

"More than I can count. It's easier now, of course. I can drive. And my dad won't touch her if I'm around. If she can get to the phone in time, I can stop him altogether. But she's always in denial. You can see his moods a mile away, but she never calls before it happens. Every time, she thinks it's going to be different."

I swallow and try to pretend that a broken porcelain frog takes all my attention. My mom never needs me and Nancy always needs him. I wonder what that would be like. I don't think it's any better. I think it's worse. She leans on him and his world weighs too much as it is.

"Where do you think he is?"

Connor shrugs. "He usually goes to his brother's for a week or so after it happens. He probably knows I'd kill him if I saw him after this."

I nod. I know he cares about his mother. I know he

wishes he could save her from Jack, that he could somehow stop it all from happening ever again.

"I just wish she would leave him. Put out a restraining order. Change the locks. She'd be so much happier."

I think so too. I can't understand how she can put up with this. How she can look at herself and think this is what she deserves.

"Yeah. Probably," I say.

I cram the rest of Nancy's broken things into the bag and then drag it out front and put it next to Connor's full one.

Tomorrow a garbage truck will come and take it away, and it will be gone forever, and Nancy will pretend it was never there at all.

Until the next time. Because if Connor's right, there will always be a next time.

February 20

FIVE MONTHS, TWENTY-ONE DAYS

Today Connor and I are out for a drive. It was his idea. He wanted out of the house. He wanted to stop thinking about the latest event in his so-called life.

I'm in the driver's seat, taking him down the most scenic, winding country roads I can find, hoping it is enough to take his mind off the bruises he saw on his mom's arms. It won't be. But I can hope.

"Wow, that's a pretty horse," I say, pointing to a splashy black and white horse in the field we pass. "Someday I'll have one. I've always wanted a horse."

That's only sort of true. I wanted one when I was little.

But I haven't thought of it in a long time. I guess I was just filling the silence.

"Yeah. It's not bad," he says, half-heartedly.

We keep driving. It's all trees and shadows and ditches. What am I supposed to talk about?

We reach a stop sign and a small colonial house sits on a grassy knoll across from us. It's not huge or fancy. In fact, the paint is peeling and one of the shutters is hanging crookedly to the side, but it's cute. "I wouldn't mind a house like that one when I'm older," I say, pointing to it. "You could do flower beds around the front walk. And the roof—"

"Don't you get it?"

The harsh tone of his voice stops me mid-sentence.

"Get what?"

"I'm not going to have any of that stuff. It might be attainable to you, but to me, it's out of reach. It will *never* happen. So stop acting like it will."

"What do you mean? We've talked about this. We're going to live in a big—"

"No. Now drop it," he growls.

I stare at him for several long moments, trying to figure out what I've done to make him so angry. He'd been fine just seconds before. Sad, yeah, but angry? It's like a switch flipping. I wish I knew what I was supposed to do. I wish I could read him better.

A car honks behind me and I'm forced to look back at the road, and I take a right turn and leave the little colonial behind. Only moments later he speaks again, and his mood has shifted a second time.

"Look, I'm sorry. It's just … sometimes I think you're too good for me. You can have anything you want. Including a house and a horse and whatever else you want. But people like me … I'm never going to have all that. My life will *always* be one big mess."

A wide spot opens up next to the road and I pull into the gravel and put the car in park. I leave the engine idling and turn toward him. "That's not true, Connor. I promise you. We'll work together and we'll get everything we've ever wanted. I swear to you, it's going to happen."

Connor doesn't seem to hear my words. He turns and stares out the window, even as it fogs over. We sit in silence on the side of the road for what seems like eternity.

And then he speaks. "When I was seven, my mom kind of lost it for a while. I don't even know where she ended up. Probably a psych ward. But I ended up with my dad for a few months without her around."

Why is he telling me this? What does it have to do with anything? Is this part of his anger or has he tipped back toward depression? Which one is worse?

"We never had much money. And with her out of the house, he had no reason to hide what he spent on alcohol. He'd buy bottles and bottles of it while the cupboards were empty. Some days I'd eat nothing but dry ramen noodles or ketchup or frozen French fries. I couldn't even cook the stuff 'cause he said I wasn't allowed."

And then it makes sense. The reason he took up cooking.

"Wow. I'm … I'm …"

What? Sorry? That doesn't seem like it's enough. I reach out, rest my hand on his shoulder. He shrugs. I don't know if he's trying to shrug my hand off or just act like it's not a big deal.

I run my hand down his arm, then reach for his hand and pull it onto my lap, interlacing my fingers with his. He's not looking at me, but the feeling of skin-on-skin somehow makes me feel better, like he knows I'm here for him.

I know he wants the stories out, but I know he also wants to act like they don't matter anymore, and he's forever stuck between hiding the pain and letting it pour out.

"I know I can't blame him for everything," he says.

"Who?" I ask, even though I know the answer.

"My dad. I mean, eventually I'm supposed to just get over it, right? I'm supposed to just say fuck it, and move on, and forget all the shitty stuff. I'm supposed to be normal and grow up and buy colonial houses with flower beds and pretty horses."

Oh. Now I get it. I take a long, slow breath, trying to figure out how I should answer, what I should think.

Because yes, sometimes I think he should just be over it. He can't blame *everything* on him, can he? He's eighteen. Old enough to take control of his life. Old enough to create his own and forget the man who screwed up everything.

But then, who am I to judge? Who am I to know what it's like? I can't even *imagine* the crap his dad has done to him. Maybe it's normal that he's haunted by it all. Maybe he's *supposed* to think about it and confront it and not just ignore it all.

"I guess," I finally say. Because that's all it is. A guess.

"That's what I want. To just put him behind me and pretend like he doesn't exist. To just ... be someone else. To work hard and to get ahead and not live *this*."

I nod my head, but I don't say anything. Sometimes the things he says ... I don't know how to answer him. I come from somewhere else. Somewhere with fancy cars and big birthday parties and Christmas sweaters and rose gardens and big screens. I'm not *this*.

"I wish I would stop fucking everything up." Connor still isn't looking at me. He's staring out the windows, as if the answer to all his problems lies somewhere in the grassy field next to my car.

For a minute I'm not sure if I heard him correctly. But then he says it again.

"I know there's a point where I'm supposed to just stop fucking everything up and look myself in the mirror and like what I see, and be my own person, and not let him be anything to me. I just wish I knew how to do that."

"Yeah. That makes sense, I guess." I stare at his hand in mine, run my finger up and down his, trying to resist the urge to trace the scars and remind him of their existence.

Am I supposed to agree, or tell him not to worry about it? And if I do agree, like I want to, if I tell him to just *get over it* and move on, is that judgmental? Will I sound too much like my mom?

The seat creaks a little as he turns to look at me, finally just *look* at me. His blue eyes are filled with such sad dejection mingled with a tiny piece of hope that it breaks my heart. "I just want ... I want us to be ... to just be. I don't want him to affect everything. I don't want to screw this up. You're the first good thing that's ever happened to me, and I don't know what to do with it." He's having a hard time talking, like the words are too heavy or too hard to get his lips around.

I stare straight into his eyes, and neither of us says a word for at least a full minute. These are the moments I fall deeper in love with him. When neither of us says anything, and we just ... *stare.* There's an understanding there that goes much deeper than words ever could. A connection so real I can't speak, because words could never say the things I feel.

"I just want you to know ... I want you to know that despite everything ... despite anything I might do or say, anything I've done before or might do in the future, I love you. More than life itself. And if some day something should happen and we're not together anymore, I'll still love you and I'll still think of you."

"Nothing like that will happen," I say. "I promise you, if you love me like I love you, nothing like that will happen."

"I know. We'll be together forever," he says. "I worship you. I love you. You're everything."

"I love you too," I say.

"Promise?"

I nod my head, slowly, solemnly. "Yes, I promise."

He kisses me, and I close my eyes and concentrate on the feeling of his lips, soft, against mine. It makes me dizzy, and I have to open my eyes.

He squeezes my hand. I don't move, just let the car idle where we sit, somewhere halfway to nowhere but not nearly far enough away from everything.

"Sometimes I think I spent forever waiting for you," he says. "My whole life, I've never had someone like you. Someone who doesn't have to be there, but is anyway. Someone who wants to just...be with me because they want me. For me. Not because I'm your brother or your kid or anything, but because you choose me."

I grip his hand tighter. "I know. My mom...sometimes I think if she could undo me, she would. If I could just somehow disappear, you know? I think I remind her of my dad, and she hates me for it."

The seat creaks again as he leans over and kisses me on the cheek. "I wish I could make all these times slow-motion, and then whenever you leave for school or work, I could fast-forward until you're back again."

And sometimes I wish that too. I wish I could control it all and fast-forward through the scary stuff.

I just wish Connor was never a part of the scary stuff.

February 13
FIVE MONTHS, FOURTEEN DAYS

Today is the anniversary of my dad's death.

For the last eight years, I have baked a cake. I'm sure to someone on the outside, it seems stupid. Like I'm baking a cake to celebrate it or something. But it's not like that.

When I was little, my dad loved cakes. Absolutely loved them. He would eat one for dinner every night if my mom let him.

I was nine the day he died. It had been coming for so long. It was like watching a freight train barrel down at you, getting closer with every second, totally unstoppable. And while my mom broke down that day and sobbed, I went a little numb. I was in denial. And so in my nine-year-old brain, I came up with the idea to just make him a cake. It made no sense then and it still doesn't now, but I like the idea of making a cake anyway.

So now it's a tradition. Each year it's gotten a little better, starting with the crappy concave disaster when I was nine to the multi-layered German chocolate I'm assembling now. I know if my dad were here, he'd cut out the biggest piece imaginable and sit down with a glass of milk and devour the whole thing.

Somehow, for this one moment, it's like he's here, and the cake is just waiting for him to walk down the stairs.

I'm not sure if I should be doing this. My mom and I don't really get along anymore, and she used to eat it with me. We never said much while we ate, but somehow there was a moment when we were both thinking about him, and it was almost as good as talking about him.

But today, it feels … like a cop-out, doing this. Like I'm going to hand her this cake and she's going to smile and we're going to have some *Leave It to Beaver* moment, and I can pretend when I leave for Connor's house that everything is perfect.

But I know it's never going to be that, because even if things go great with Connor and she miraculously starts accepting him, I remember the things she's said. They're like a wedge between us, and the words can't be taken back.

But I'm making this cake anyway, because if I don't, it's like ignoring my dad. It's like pretending he never existed. And my mom does that enough for both of us.

My mom gets home from work at six, and she walks past the kitchen and then does a double take when she sees me sitting on a stool, the cake towering in front of me.

"Hi," I say. "It's German chocolate this year."

She just stares at it for a long, silent moment, and I'm not sure what she's thinking, if she's happy or touched or just angry that I would even try to do something like this after the fights we've been having.

Sometimes I think I might just march right up to her and say *I love you*, right to her face, just to see if she says it back.

A month ago, I stood in the hall outside her room. And I really wanted to do it. I really thought about it. But no matter how many times I reached out to her door, I couldn't get my fingers to grip that brass doorknob. There were too many other arguments, too many hurtful words between us to say it now.

And so that six-paneled slab stayed between us.

"Thank you," she says, her voice quiet. "That was very nice of you."

And then she shocks me, because she crosses the room and she hugs me, at this awkward angle because I'm sitting on a stool.

But she doesn't let me go, she just keeps hugging me. And so I stand and hug her back, and she just hugs tighter and tighter, and neither of us speak for such a long, silent moment it seems to stretch on forever.

It's too hard to break. The silence is too heavy, too firm, to break with those three words, even though now seems like the time to do it. The words are lodged in my mouth, though. They won't come out.

And then she sniffles and pulls away. "Can you put that in the fridge? I think I'll take a hot bath."

Her voice comes out choked and gargled and I don't have time to say anything before she's walking up the steps.

What just happened?

February 7

Connor got a new job. He's gone today, and I am alone. After months of it being him and me all the time, I don't know what to do with myself. I have time and quiet and silence.

My mom had something to do in Seattle today, almost three hours away, so I'm in my room, lying on the plush carpet and staring at the glowing stars I put up years ago. It's hard to know who I was then. When stickers and coloring books ruled the day.

I like my room. It is my Eden. Even though the door is just some fake hollow-core one, it seems like a fortress in here and nothing can get in.

When my phone rings, I almost don't recognize it. Those big red lips make a funny shrill sound. I haven't been home to hear this ring in a long time. I'm always slipping through that door past eleven o'clock, hoping today isn't the day my mom cracks down on my curfew.

I get up and grab it. It must be Connor. I wonder how his first day is going.

But it is not.

It's Abby.

"Ann?"

I freeze. Her voice is so familiar and so ... foreign at the same time.

"H-Hi," I say.

"I can't believe you answered."

"Yeah. I'm home today."

"Do you want to do something?"

Her question hangs in the air for a long time. All I can hear is the buzzing in the receiver. I think she might have hung up. "Yes," I finally answer. And it is the truth.

"I'll be there in twenty."

And she hangs up before I can change my mind.

———

Twenty minutes later, we're racing down the back roads in her yellow Mustang. Abby and I used to be completely obsessed with Christina Aguilera, even though she's kind of lame now and it's totally embarrassing. But we like Classic Christina, like "Genie in a Bottle" classic. And we shout it at the top of our lungs as the wind whips through her car. Even though it's a cold February day, we leave the windows down as the chill tangles our hair and makes our throats sore.

Freedom. That is what I feel today. That is all I feel right now.

Abby and I end up at Red Robin, where we order overpriced fruity drinks and bottomless baskets of fries.

We will eat until we want to explode.

"Did you hear that Jan Nichols is dating Mike Fenser?" Abby holds out the shaker of seasoning salt and I douse my French fries in it and pass it back.

"Eww!"

"I know." She grins, her eyes sparkling. Abby has always loved gossip, and it's been so long since we've had time to talk like this. "He's, like, totally gross and sweaty." She sticks out her tongue, as if the idea of making out with Mike Fenser is the most disgusting thing she's ever heard.

"And huge," I say. I puff up my chest and scrunch my shoulders up. "He doesn't even have a neck. His chin just blends right into his pecs."

Abby's eyes flare and she laughs, this amazing, loud, totally *Abby* way to laugh. "And she's, like, tiny. Can you imagine them..." Abby says as she mimes a hip thrust.

"Eww!" I say again, faking a dry heave.

Abby takes a bite of her burger, but it all falls apart in her basket. She doesn't seem to mind, and she picks up the pieces with her fingers and pops them in her mouth. "I guess they hooked up at Winter Formal or something."

Winter Formal. I try not to let those two words hit me like they do, but I can't keep that twinge of bitterness away as I think of the emerald dress hanging in the closet where no one has ever seen it. I set my burger back down in the basket because it's suddenly very hard to swallow.

I take a long, slow drink of my strawberry lemonade, but it doesn't taste as good as it did three minutes ago.

Abby seems to know she shouldn't have said those two words because she changes the subject. Too quickly. "Do you want to go see that new Jennifer Garner movie? It's supposed to be really funny."

I glance at my watch. Connor will be off in two hours, which isn't enough time to see the movie and get home. He said he would call me on his way there, and I know he will.

But even with the awkward Winter Formal moment, I'm having too much fun to stop now. Connor won't mind about a movie. He knows I never see Abby.

"Yes. Absolutely. Let's do it."

Abby grins excitedly. Twenty minutes later we leave Red Robin and walk across the mall parking lot to the theater, where she buys us two tickets and a tub of popcorn big enough to feed six people.

For two hours I lose myself in a romantic comedy that makes me think of Connor at all the right moments and makes me forget life at the same time. By the time we leave, I feel lighter than air. I think I float to the car.

Today was exactly what I needed. Why have I been avoiding Abby so much? Why don't I just balance my life instead of giving it all to Connor? He loves me, and I love him, but we should do other things with other people sometimes too. We don't have to be so wrapped up in our relationship.

I'm excited to see Connor, so I have Abby take me directly there. I'll have him drop me off at my house later. I want to see how his day went.

When we pull up and I see Connor sitting on the porch, my heart jams into my throat. Why is he sitting out here in the dead of winter? It's cold enough to see your breath.

He stands up and walks toward us, and I can tell just by the way he's walking that he's angry. His feet fall in a heavy rhythm, his strides so long his legs are stretching to eat up the ground.

My heart sinks. I shouldn't have turned off my phone in the theater. I shouldn't have watched the movie at all. Not when I promised him I'd be waiting for him when he got home. I'm over an hour late. He might have had things he wanted to tell me about his first day.

Or he might just have been worried about me—

"Where have you been?"

He's at the door as I get out of the car. "Abby and I saw a movie—"

"You said you'd be here when I got home. My whole day was crazy, and then I get here—"

I don't even realize that Abby has gotten out of the car until she is next to me. "God, relax. We went and saw a movie. I think you can survive without her for one damn afternoon."

I open my mouth to tell Abby to let me handle it, but I can't get a word out before he does.

"Stay out of it," he says, turning his attention to Abby. I grab his arm. I don't need this confrontation.

Abby stands directly in front of him. "She's my best friend. I don't need to stay out of it. In fact, maybe I've stayed out of it too long. Maybe I should have told her what I really thought the day I met you, huh?"

Connor's eyes narrow and he pulls his arm away from me. "Maybe I should have told her what I thought of *you.*"

"Oh, please. I'd love to hear it. What's your beef with me? Am I too nice? Because you're a pretty big ass. Or maybe I'm too smart? Because you're pretty stupid."

I cringe. Of all the words, why did she choose *stupid*? He hates that word.

He steps toward her, closing the gap in less than a second. But she doesn't move. She's taller than me. Tall enough that she can almost look him in the eye.

"I'm not afraid of you. You think you're tough but you're not." She stares at him, a gleam of confidence and arrogance in her eyes. She's enjoying the confrontation, as much as she can, anyway. She's been waiting for this moment. Now I realize it. She's been biting her tongue all this time, waiting for her chance to tell him what she thinks.

She turns away from him and puts her hand over mine, where it rests on the car door. "Don't stay here, Ann. Come with me. You don't deserve this."

All I can do is stare at her hand on mine. I'm frozen.

"I can't. You know I can't," I say in a whisper, as if I hope Connor won't hear.

"No. You can." She whispers too, but even as she says it, her hand slides off of mine. "But you won't."

I look up at her and she stares at me, straight in the eyes, and no words pass between us. But she understands it. She's not mad. I don't know how she does it, but she's not mad at me. She just nods and gives me a fast hug, flips Connor off, and returns to the driver's seat.

Connor tries to pull me away but I just stand at the curb and watch her yellow Mustang disappear around the corner.

Some part of me feels like this might be the last time I ever see her.

February 5
FIVE MONTHS, SIX DAYS

It was a half day at school today, but I forgot until second period. Connor wasn't home when I went by his house, so I ended up back at home again.

Which is weird. More and more, I just sleep in my bed and that's it. I don't have dinner here, I don't watch TV, I just come home and fall into bed.

But today I'm sitting on the couch, catching a *Gossip Girl* rerun and painting my toenails even though it's winter and no one will see them. I've eaten half a bag of Doritos. It's an oddly comforting afternoon.

But then I hear the garage door hum open. I know my mom has arrived, and all that tranquility floods out faster than it arrived.

I haven't seen her in about two weeks. I know she's going to ask where I've been every day, what I'm up to. How my grades are. She may not be loving, but she's predictable.

I cap the nail polish and use a piece of newspaper to fan my nails. I hear her heels click across the Travertine-tiled kitchen and I know she hears the movie on.

"Oh, Ann! What are you doing home?" I look up to see her generic three-piece suit in forest green, and her hair pulled up in its usual no-nonsense French twist.

I shrug. "Teacher in-service or something."

She nods. "How is school going?"

"Good. I think I got a 3.7 this semester."

She nods. "That's great. Are you having trouble in any of your courses? Your teachers being fair?"

I shrug. "Everything's fine."

"And your boyfriend? How is he?"

"Good."

She moves and is sitting next to me on the couch before I can blink.

"Are you sure he's not..." her voice trails off.

"Not what?"

"I just think... I think there are other fish in the sea," she says, all in one breath, like a big *woosh* of words. I wonder how long she's been saving that, looking for the right moment.

I shrug. "I'm sure there are. But I want to be with him."

"Why, though? It's not like—"

This time she stops abruptly.

"It's not like what?" I ask.

"He's not really..." her voice trails off yet again.

"Just tell me what you're trying to say." My voice comes out a little rougher than I'd meant it to because I just want her to spit it out already, and it's obvious it's not going to be good. Why beat around the bush?

"He's not good enough," she says. "For you. You're better than him."

And there it is. Her opinion, right out in the open. I knew she didn't like him. Even when she was smiling at him that day she met him, I could see something behind it. She was trying too hard to be nice and cheerful. It wasn't real.

"There's more to him than you see," I tell her.

"Enlighten me," she says, her voice a little too terse. She's sitting so perfectly next to me, her back ramrod straight.

"He's not on trial, Mom. I'm not going to debate it with you."

"I just think you need to meet other people," she says, reaching out to pat my knee. It's hard not to jerk it away. It's hard not to snap right back at her, because I hate that she wants to force us apart. He's the love of my life. I'm not leaving him. Not now, not ever. I promised him. No matter what.

"Mom, just stop, okay? Not going to happen."

And then I reach for the nail polish but only succeed in knocking it over, and it pools over the wooden side table, a big splotch of red.

"Just think about it. Aim higher."

And then, before I can say anything coherent in response, she's gone and I'm left cleaning up the mess.

January 30
FIVE MONTHS

My hair is piled atop my head in curls and I have a pretty necklace around my neck. A little diamond pendant Connor bought me two weeks ago.

But I'm all dressed up with nowhere to go. Just sitting on the couch near the door, waiting.

I don't know where he is.

I'm not sure I want to know. Maybe it's better if he never calls to tell me, and I just sit here and wonder.

His dad has been on a drinking binge for two days, and I know that is the problem. I know he's off somewhere dealing with it, dealing with his mom, trying to sort out the problems that never leave him.

I know Abby is going to figure it out. She's going to look everywhere for me. She'll stand at the door to the gym and watch expectantly for me to round the corner in the beautiful green dress she helped pick out.

But I'll just be sitting here, waiting for him, and he'll never show up.

I don't know why I thought this would work. Why I thought Connor could do something... *teen* like this.

Connor lives in a world made for people much older than his eighteen years. He lives in a world that ages him faster than is fair.

It's why I feel as if I've been with him for years and not months. Because everything is accelerated and intense and real, and high school dances are childish and silly and pointless.

But I still wanted this. I'm still near tears as I sit here, with my forty-dollar updo and my newly polished nails.

An hour in the salon chair, and no one's even going to see my hair.

The disappointment tastes bitter. Tonight he was going to talk with Abby and laugh with me, and for once it was going to be different. Things were going to be like I thought they were going to be when I met him five months ago. He was going to be a piece that fit into my life and made it whole, not the piece that forced the rest of it all apart.

Connor wanted to take me to this, wanted to be there for me, and his father ruined it, and he has to save his mom even though she will never save herself.

And yet I still wait, as the night sky darkens and the

house goes quiet. It is not until eleven, when the dance is over, that I go back to my room and slip off my dress, hang it back in the closet where no one will ever see it. I shove it far back to ensure that, because maybe if I never see it again I won't remember how this feels.

I sit at my vanity and pull the pins from my hair, watching as it tumbles down around my shoulders. I wipe my face clean of the makeup I'd so painstakingly applied and I climb into my bed, my skin still tingling with the cleanser.

Winter Formal has come and gone, and I was not there to see it.

August 30
ONE YEAR

I listen to Connor plead with me through the door, my forehead still resting on my knees, my eyes closed.

He must be getting soaked out there. Knowing him, he's not even wearing a jacket—probably just a thermal underneath a T-shirt.

Thunder rumbles from somewhere distant, grows louder, and then disappears again.

Connor is shouting to be heard over the storm.

I lift my head up and look at the window, and watch the rivulets of water streaming down the glass. I wish it was as easy to wash away the pain.

He lowers his voice a little as he pleads with me. "I promise you. I swear, I will never do this again. I'll get help this time. I went too far, I know. I'll go to anger management or counseling or something. Anything. Please, Ann, just let me in. Let me take care of you. I need you."

I rest my forehead on my knees again.

I know he needs me.

That's the problem.

He needs me to fight away the wars he wages with himself. He needs me to hold him together so he doesn't crack right in half.

I used to think I could do it.

I don't anymore. People don't change because you want them to. They aren't clay, ready to be molded.

Connor might as well be steel for all the good my efforts did.

The only one who changed was me.

It's been so long since I walked around smiling, laughing, holding my head up high. So long since I've looked forward to the future. So long since I even dreamt of a future at all, one beyond rain clouds and fights and never-ending gray.

And if I open the door right now, it'll always be that way.

Unless...

Unless this is rock bottom. He has to know, now, that getting anger management and counseling is the only option left.

He hurt me. It isn't just a bruise this time. I think something is broken. My entire body throbs.

I close my eyes tighter and wish that the sound of his voice on the other side of the door wasn't so loud inside my head.

I've survived so far. And I have a choice to make.

I have to decide who I love more: me or Connor.

January 20

FOUR MONTHS, TWENTY-ONE DAYS

Connor's parents are out this afternoon, and so we take full advantage of it, spreading the newspaper and applications and resumes all over the floor, trying to decide the best plan of action. Organization has never really been my forte, but today I'm equipped with high-lighters and sticky notes and a legal pad.

Our mission, should we choose to accept it, is to get Connor a job. A decent one, not a minimum wage one like he's had before. Those jobs aren't making an impression on his savings account.

He wants to move out. Bad. So we're going to find

something that pays enough for him to get out of his parents' house, and once he's in his own place, everything is going to change. Finally, we can put them behind us. It will just be us and we can forget the things they've done to him, and he'll just think of me and our future. Nothing will touch us.

I pick up a piece of the classifieds. "What about this? *'Day laborer wanted. Busy construction co seeks hard worker. Starts at nine dollars an hour.'*"

He wrinkles his nose. "I don't know ... nine bucks isn't much if it's hard work."

I shrug. My mom only makes me work in the summer, and even then, I think it's just to keep me busy while she works. She puts half my money into savings for college and I spend the other half on whatever I want. I've never really had to *labor*. I guess I can't judge him for that.

"Okay, how 'bout this one? *'Electricians Assistant. Pay DOE, some experience preferred.'* I mean, you don't have experience really, but if they don't get anyone good they might give you a shot."

He shrugs and I know he's not into it. I guess it's kind of a long shot. Connor doesn't have much job experience, just some short stints at a couple restaurants and some summer work at a landscaping company. All the drama at home kind of ruins his reliability, and people don't really care what problems you have, they just want you to show up every single day as if you haven't spent all night keeping peace between your mom and dad.

I hand him the paper. "Okay, well, look through here and I'll work on the applications then. My writing is neater."

And so I pick up the first one, for a hardware store, and I painstakingly print his name, birthday, address, and phone number. It's all memorized.

When I get to *Reason for leaving last position* I have to get a little creative. For the landscaping position, I print *No opportunities for advancement.* It's mostly true and I'm sure no one will ask. What kind of opportunities could there be? He mowed lawns all summer.

The whole thing is an exercise in creative writing. By the time I get to the end, I'm not sure if there are more truths or lies. But they're only white lies and omissions, and he needs a job to get away from here.

Once he's been at the new job for a while, he'll have a whole new history and he'll be able to move up and forget all these silly little things. We're going to rewrite his past, one year at a time. Once I'm out of college, we'll both have clean slates and bright futures. It'll be perfect.

I didn't manage to apply to UW like I'd always planned, so it looks like I'll start off by going to community college. I haven't said anything to Connor yet, but sometimes I want to ask him if he'll go with me, take a few classes and build something for himself. Maybe it would give him something to look forward to.

By the time we're done, I have six applications written in neat little block letters, and four more places to drop resumes off. My hand is aching, but I feel good about this.

Connor's mood lifts once he sees our progress and realizes that maybe a new job will be reality. I realize all I have to do is show him how to put his dreams into practice, put things into motion, and he'll see how easy it is. He doesn't have to just dream, he can do it. Nothing can stop him.

Nothing can stop us.

December 15

THREE MONTHS, FIFTEEN DAYS

I grab the last of my textbooks from my locker, and when I slam the door and see Abby standing on the other side, staring straight at me, I'm so shocked I jump back.

"Oh, God, you scared me. Don't do that."

I laugh, but she doesn't join in. She just keeps staring, that solemn look on her face.

"Is it that shocking to see your best friend?" she asks.

It should be a joke, but it's not.

"I know you called me yesterday. I'm sorry." I stare down at my books. "I was going to call you." When did I grab the physics text? I don't need that one.

I turn back to the lock and start spinning it, looking

for number thirty-two. I don't know why, but I feel like I've done something wrong. Like she caught me with my hand in the cookie jar or something.

"I called last week, too. And the week before." There should be an edge in her voice, but there's not. I don't think she has it in her to be mad at me, even if I am ignoring her. She steps closer to me. "We're supposed to turn in the outline for our project in three days and it's only half done."

I swallow and keep staring at the numbers on the dial, but I swing right past six and have to start over. Guilt wells up in my stomach.

I shouldn't keep avoiding her like this. Abby and I were inseparable three months ago.

Three months. That's how long I've been with Connor, and that's how long it takes to forget what it's like to hang out with your best friend every day.

I take my eyes off the lock and look at her. She's so close I can see right into her pupils. It's almost worse to realize she's not angry, just hurt. I shouldn't keep abandoning her like this.

"We can do something. Soon. Email me the outline and I'll add to it."

"That's what you said about the resources page. I had to complete it myself during math class because you forgot."

I cringe. "I know. I've been a crappy friend. We'll work on it soon, I swear."

God, what is wrong with this stupid lock?

"How 'bout tonight?"

I stop on thirty-two again. I knew she'd ask that. It's

why I have such a hard time talking to her now. It used to be every night we'd hang out. No notice, no asking, we just knew. So when Connor came along, I disrupted all that.

But all I think of all day is hanging out with him, seeing him, and it's what I want most. How can I tell her that?

I can't. "Call me tomorrow and we can get together. We'll get a bunch of junk food and catch up on the project. Maybe we can even get ahead, you know? I'll stay all night, I promise."

I get my locker open and cram the physics book inside it and then slam it closed and turn toward her. I hate the look on her face as my words register. I hate that I'm putting her off again. But Connor already told me he has a surprise for me tonight. And he said he was thinking about hanging out on the beach this weekend. I'm just booked up, is all. I really do want to hang out with her, just not right this minute.

"Okay. Fine."

"Okay?"

I don't know why I ask again. Why I think if she *says* it's okay, it really is.

"Sure. See you later," she says, then turns and walks away before I can say anything else.

And as I watch her retreat, I wonder how long I can keep ignoring her before she no longer considers me a friend.

December 10

THREE MONTHS, TEN DAYS

I've come to expect his calls. I've turned down my phone so the ringer can't be heard outside my bedroom door, and then I leave it on the windowsill, just on the other side of my pillow.

If he calls, I will answer before the first ring has gone silent. And my mom won't hear it.

Sometimes I don't sleep well, waiting for it. Waiting for the phone to scream in my ear, and my heart to thunder to a roar as I go from dreamland to reality in a half second.

I'm prepared when it rings. I grab at the phone and when I pick it up, the buttons light up the dark. "Hello?"

My voice is not groggy. It never is. No matter when he calls, I'm always wide awake for him.

"Ann?"

I don't have to read the tone of his voice to know his mood. It is 1:50 a.m. He only calls at this time because he's depressed. Because he needs me.

"Yeah. I'm here."

I roll over onto my back and blink into the darkness.

"I'm not... I can't handle this anymore."

His words sit there. I don't respond for a long time. I just blink some more and stare into the darkness. I know that is the wrong thing to do, but I don't want to say the wrong words. "Talk to me."

"It's just not... I just can't handle this. I have nothing."

"You have me," I say. "And I love you."

"I know, but I'm so tired of this. You have no idea, I'm so tired of this."

Me too.

"Just talk to me, okay? You have a lot to think about. Your uncle set you up with that interview. And if it doesn't work out, we'll get a newspaper and apply for every job in the classified section. You'll be able to move out soon. I promise. It will get better."

"I wish I'd grown up in your world. I wish he didn't exist."

"You can't change the past. You can only change the future."

"I know. But sometimes I don't know how to do that.

I'm just going to repeat history. I'm just going to be a loser like him."

"No. You're smarter than him. You know you are. You'll be a success. You'll go so far."

I don't know what to say to him during these conversations. I've said every version of everything I can think of. It used to be that just talking to me was enough. His mood would shift a soon as I answered the phone.

But more and more, I have to talk him into it. More and more, I have to be clever and smart and I have to lead him down the path to get him to see it.

"I want to walk to the bridge," he says. The words break through my daze as if he literally shook me awake. There's no threat in his voice. Just a promise. Just reality.

I sit up in bed and wrap the blanket around my shoulders. "Don't do this, please."

"I have nothing, Ann. You don't understand."

"Just don't do this," I repeat. "You have so much. You know you do."

He sniffles. I know he's crying. Even though there are times he seems whole, the cracks still show. And today they are spreading and splintering, and today he may crumble.

"If I come over, will you wait for me?"

The silence is deafening. I think I may have lost him already.

"I'll wait for you."

"Be there in ten."

And I hang up before he can argue, before he can change his mind. I find yesterday's clothes and pull them on, but take my time opening my door. My mom's bedroom is on the opposite end of the hall. I can hear her snore.

She has no idea.

I slip down the stairs and write a note on the notepad on the fridge. "Went to school early. Cramming for Lit class."

I know my mom will get up at six thirty. I know it doesn't make sense that I'd be gone by then to go cram for a class, but I don't care.

And I know she will know. But she can't prove it. And sometimes I think she'd rather just believe everything is perfect than question it all and admit it's not. Her way of dealing has always been avoidance.

Our driveway is sloped, so I let out the emergency brake and my car glides backward into the street. And then I start it up and drive away.

My car is silent. I don't touch the radio or the heat; I just shiver in the quiet as I pass under the streetlamps and past all the dark houses. I wonder what everyone else is doing right now. I wonder if they are warm and secure in their beds, if they know things like this are happening all around them.

When I arrive at his house, the front door is unlocked, and I slip back to his room, past his parents' door.

He's lying in his bed, the radio playing a haunting piano melody. For a moment I just stand at the door and stare, because he isn't moving and I think he might be asleep. But then I see him move and rub his eyes.

I walk to his bed and slide in and he turns to me, and

he wraps his arms around me and buries his face in my hair. I let out a long sigh, and the tension leaves my body.

We don't speak. We just fall asleep. All he needed was for me to be here, and he can relax and sleep.

And tomorrow he will forget all of this. Tomorrow he will be himself again, and we can forget all this and just be together.

And even if I have to do this many more times until things get better, I'll do it, because I love him, and it makes a difference in his life.

Together, we're unstoppable.

November 21

TWO MONTHS, TWENTY-TWO DAYS

When I arrive at Connor's house today, his stereo is so loud I have to cover both ears with my hands as I walk down the hall toward his room. When I open the door, it's even louder. The sounds flood my senses, a bass-heavy rock sound.

When I swing his bedroom door open, Connor whirls on me so fast I stumble backward. I see the flash of anger in his eyes before it changes. Before he realizes it's just me.

His mouth drops, and he pulls me close so I can hear what he says. He has to shout over the music. "Oh God, I'm sorry, I thought you were my dad." He wraps his arms around me. "I didn't mean to scare you."

I wriggle away from him. This is just weird. He looks into my eyes, and I know I must look worried because he gives me the "one minute" signal and goes to the stereo. The sounds stop abruptly. My ears ring in the silence.

I wait for him to explain what's going on.

"It's been a long day." Connor sinks into the little recliner in his room, but I just stand there, near the door. I'm still a little off-kilter from that look he gave me. From the anger that swarmed in his eyes. He was someone else. Someone I've never seen before.

I hit things, not people. That's what he told me. But for just a second there, it was like he could hit someone. Not me. But maybe his dad.

"Do you want to talk about it?"

Connor lets loose with a long, slow sigh. "I don't know. I mean, do you really want to know it all? I told you my life is just…messed up."

I step further into the room. "Tell me. It'll make you feel better."

He purses his lips for a second. He's holding back, not sure if I can handle it. I can. I know I can. If he'd just let me help.

"My dad took a bunch of my mom's favorite pictures and ripped them all up."

"Why?"

"My mom wanted to go away for the weekend and see her mom. My grandma's sick or something. He said she was choosing sides."

"Oh."

I say that word too much around him. It's always *oh*. Why don't I ever know what to say? Why can't I just fix everything by making him see that his dad doesn't matter anymore?

Connor interlaces his hands into a steeple, but then starts twisting them around, full of nervous energy. Or is it fury? I'm still not sure.

"He doesn't have the right to do that to her. To take everything and just destroy it like that. It's her mom. And she's old. She could die of whatever it is, and he doesn't want to let her go see her." His voice is quieter now. I think the anger has gone.

I walk up to him so that I'm standing right in front of the chair, our knees are almost touching. "You're right. That's screwed up."

Connor gives me a sad, pathetic little smile, but he doesn't look me in the eyes. "I told ya you didn't want to know all this."

"But I do. I want to know everything about you. No secrets."

Connor looks back at his hands and nods. I can almost see the relief, that he's happy I haven't turned and run straight out the door. "My dad takes everything from everyone. He wants it all. If he can't be happy, you can't either. He's done it to me hundreds of times. You find something that you love, something that makes you happy, and he'll destroy it."

He finally looks up at me, and I realize it's just sadness—no anger, no fury. He reaches up and tugs on the loop on my jeans, and I sit on his lap, so that my side is against his chest, and I lean until I'm curled into him and he puts his arms around my waist. He's warm, his breath hot on my neck.

His voice gets quieter now that I'm closer. "He got a dog once, a beagle. I loved him. Named him Peanut. But once he realized how much the dog meant to me, he got rid of it. I have no idea if he gave it away or shot it or what. It was just gone. I cried for a week." He starts tracing circles on my back. "It's so hard to live like this. To have this constant turmoil. I just want it to be over. I want it to be all over."

Something in his voice isn't right. It's like he's not saying he wants the turmoil to be over, but that he wants his *life* to be over. I take my time answering him. All the words are important. It's about so much more than what he's saying.

"It will be, eventually. You won't live with it forever. You'll find a job soon, and you can move out and leave it all behind."

I stare at us in the mirrored closet doors, at him with his face against my neck, at me just sitting there, a tired, pained look on my face. It's such a miserable little portrait that I want to march across the house and go scream at his father for screwing everything up.

"I've been saying that to myself for years. I've been thinking it for years. But it's never over. I can never walk away from it. My mom needs my help. All the time. Why do you think he's gone right now? I had to get in his face for him to back down. It will never end. I just want it all over."

There it is again. What is he saying?

I close my eyes, because I don't want to look at our reflection anymore, and concentrate on the soothing feeling of his palm on the back of my knit top, on the feeling of his breath on my skin.

"I know," I say, even though I don't. Even though I have no idea what he's talking about.

"Sometimes I just want to … I just want to …"

His voice trails off. I don't think he'll finish it. "I'm just so depressed I want to end it all. My life."

And there it is. The statement that's been between the lines all along is finally out there.

I sit more upright so I can turn and look at him. *Implore* him. "Don't say that. I love you. Things will get better, I promise."

"But how can they? I'm stuck with this. It's what I was born into and it's what I'll die as. Surrounded by it."

I'm shaking my head before he's even done talking. Can't he see? He doesn't have to be this forever. "Yeah, but you have me now. We'll get through it together. I'll help you. I promise you. I'm here to stay."

It's so stupid, what I'm saying. But he looks up at me and one side of his mouth lifts in the tiniest smile. It doesn't reach his eyes, but it's still a smile. "You're so good to me."

And I smile back at him and he pulls me closer, kissing

my neck, my collarbone, my arm, and I know I've said the right thing.

But even as we get lost in our kiss, I can't erase the image of the anger flashing in his eyes. It was foreign. It didn't belong there.

He's not like that.

November 19

TWO MONTHS, TWENTY DAYS

Connor and I are playing another board game today. This time it's Battleship. I'm terrible at it. He's sunk three of mine and I have yet to land a hit. He's good at all these games and I'm always terrible. But for some reason I still love every minute of it.

"B-7," I say, picking up a white peg.

"Miss."

"Oh, how ever did I know? I think you're cheating."

"Am not."

I set my game board down on the hardwood and sit up on my knees and try to look over at his board, but he tips it away from me. "Now look who's trying to cheat!"

"I swear you're moving your boats or you didn't put them on there at all. How can I have zero hits so far? That defies the laws of probability."

"I'm just good at this," he says, grinning at me with a toothy smile.

"I don't believe you."

And then I launch after him and he's so surprised he falls over, and before I know it I'm straddling him and we're wrestling with his board.

"No fair—I can't hurt you!" He's grinning and loving every minute of this, just like I am.

"So? You don't play fair anyway."

He rolls me over so fast I hardly blink before I'm pinned under him and the board is forgotten. The television is still on in the background, casting hazy blue light around us. His eyes are so intense I could get lost in them all night, but then he's kissing me and I close mine again.

Every night, we get closer to the moment. Every night, I step closer to the edge.

And tonight I'm ready to jump. I was ready before, but nervous, and I've thought about it long enough. I don't just *think* I'm ready, I *am* ready.

He pulls a blanket over us both, on the ground, and I lose all sense of time, but somehow it's just us and the blanket, skin on skin in our warm little cocoon.

He looks straight at me, his eyes piercing mine, and I nod at him. I can't say it. Not out loud.

But he knows. He reaches a hand outside the blanket,

pulls something from the nightstand, and is back with me again.

"Are you sure?" he whispers as he settles back on top of me.

And I nod again and watch his eyes darken like a storm cloud, and then I squeeze my eyes shut.

After tonight, there will be nothing left in between us.

That is the way I want it.

"I love you," I say.

"I love you too," he whispers, his breath hot in my ear.

For a second, when it happens, there is a burst of pain and I squeeze my knees together, even though he's between them and it won't do me any good.

He freezes. "Are you okay?"

I don't talk for a moment, the breath stolen from my lungs, but then the pain ebbs and I nod. "Yes. Just go slow," I say, my voice hoarse.

He kisses my cheek, my temple, my ear, and finally my lips, and then he eases back a little before going forward, and I tense for a moment, but it doesn't hurt anymore, and I breathe normally again.

As he picks up a rhythm, his breath quickens and so does my own, and our blanket cocoon quickly warms, until we have to pull it back.

I almost don't recognize the low, quiet growl that tears loose from the back of his throat, but I know what it means when he collapses on top of me, his breath still coming in heavy gasps.

After a few seconds in silence, he pulls back and looks

at me, a sheepish blush spreading from his hairline to his lips. "I'm sorry I…I mean, that wasn't…I'm sorry that wasn't—uh—longer lasting."

And then I can't help it. I burst out laughing. I have to push him off my chest because my stomach hurts, I laugh so hard.

"That wasn't supposed to be funny," he says, even though he's chuckling now, too.

"I know, it's just, the look on your face…"

I manage to stop laughing long enough to kiss him.

"And I really…that was perfect. I promise."

"It wasn't. But I'll get better. *I* promise."

"If you're lucky I might just let you prove it."

November 7

TWO MONTHS, EIGHT DAYS

Abby's birthday is today. I've spent half the day getting ready, throwing a dozen outfits all over the floor of my room and wriggling in and out of every skirt, pair of jeans, and slacks I own. We have a table for six at the Seattle Space Needle; we are going into the city and we will be dining in style, and I can't decide what's appropriate to wear. For some reason it seems inordinately important.

It feels weird to plan something without Connor. We've only been together for two months, but I spend every single day at his house, watching as the clock counts down toward my curfew.

And even though I wish I was with him right now,

I'm also excited to see Abby. We haven't hung out in, like, two weeks, and it's mostly my fault. I don't want to totally abandon her.

Abby is the kind of friend everyone wants. The kind who remembers your birthday and helps you study for a test and loans you her car if yours breaks down even though she had a date, so you can go on one of your own.

Abby is just … Abby. There's no one like her. She moved here from Texas so it might be some Southern hospitality thing or something, I don't know. But thanks to her, I picture all Texans like this, with a Southern drawl and a charming selflessness. I'm sure if I ever actually went to Texas I'd be disappointed, because there's no way the rest of them could live up to her.

She's never missed a birthday of mine since she moved here freshman year, so I can't miss hers.

I slip a cute flowery blouse over my head and survey the results in the mirror. The jeans are too casual, so I slide on a pair of khakis and give it one more perusal. Not bad. I dig a sweater out of my closet in case it gets cold later.

I hear a horn, so I glance out the window to see Abby stepping out of a limo. It's her eighteenth, so her parents are going all out. I take the stairs two by two and I'm at the door before she can ring the bell.

"Happy birthday!" I hug her and hand her my gift. "You have to wait 'til dinner, though."

"You look cute!" Abby leads me to the limo and a man in the typical driver's uniform opens the door. She motions toward the car as if she's Vanna White. "Your limo awaits, darling!"

I laugh as I slide across the polished leather seats. I can't help but sigh as everything melts away. This night is exactly what I need.

"So we have to pick up Jessica, Rachel, and Janelle and then we're headed out. Want a drink?"

It's sparkling cider, and even though it feels childish to pretend it's champagne, we do anyway, clinking our glasses and toasting Abby's eighteenth. And so it goes, as we chat and catch up and pick up the rest of the guests along the way, and it's like nothing has ever come between us. It's like I haven't ignored her for the past few weeks. I want to apologize for it, I want to explain, but doing so makes it seem like I'm pushing it in her face on her birthday. So I don't.

The city lights sparkle as we approach downtown, the towers jutting into the darkening skyline. I feel the tiniest twinge of regret as I see the glimmer of the lights, wishing Connor was here with me to see it. It's incredibly romantic.

Once we've driven for what seems like eternity, the limo pulls into a big circular turn-around and we all get out and walk to the foot of the Needle, our heels clicking on the walk. I feel sophisticated, like we all belong here. Like we do this every day or something.

The elevator access is inside a gift shop filled with a zillion different replications of the Space Needle. I resist the urge to shop for a souvenir of this night, and our group fills the lift and the door slides shut.

There's an actual elevator operator, which is a first for

me. He's wearing this jaunty cap and silly tux and talking about the origin of the place—something about the World's Fair—but I'm not listening, because I can't stop looking out the glass walls. The elevator carries us upward, into the night, and I watch as the lights of the city sparkle below us. Our view gets bigger and bigger, until I can see Puget Sound and downtown and everything in between.

Once inside the restaurant, they usher us to a table near the window. Abby and I get the best seats, near the glass.

A waitress with fiery red hair walks up and hands us leather-bound menus. Everything looks so good. Stuffed chicken breast and rack of lamb and even elk. Who wants elk? That sounds gross. I decide to stick with chicken. If it's good, I'll tell Connor about it and we'll look up recipes and try to make it at home. Maybe I'll even buy some of that sparkling cider and we can make our own romantic meal.

The waitress comes back with strawberry lemonade for all of us, real strawberries bobbing amongst the ice.

Janelle reaches for hers and knocks it right over, and the ice cubes slide across the table and land in Rachel's lap.

My body tenses as I watch it pool over the white linens, and I wait for someone to freak out, to yell or jump back from the table. But nothing happens.

And I don't know why I thought it would. No one cares. Abby just laughs and says something about how she can't believe Janelle is coordinated enough to make the cheer squad.

And then we order, and we watch the night sky as it continually rolls by, the whole dining room revolving so that our view changes. It takes an hour for us to see everything, but it's not enough.

I want to see more. I want to stay up here all night and count every twinkling light downtown, and I want it to never end.

October 29

I don't have a good feeling about this. Even though I love him, I don't think my mom will see it. I don't think she will see past his rough exterior to understand what I love about him.

Connor isn't good with strangers. He gets anxiety, and instead of blabbing like an idiot—like I do when I get nervous—he keeps his mouth shut. And then people think he's rude, but he's just misunderstood. He really is a nice guy, they just misjudge him, is all.

I know my mom thought I was going to run off to some Ivy League school and marry a guy who rows boats and wears sweaters. I've always had decent grades, and I do want to go to college. But Ivy League? Yeah, right. I'm not exactly an overachiever. Just an achiever. Good grades, track, the usual.

But I want her to like him, even if he doesn't fit what she's imagined. I want her to see in him what I see, and I want her to give her approval. I want her to know I'm going to be okay. Maybe that will help her. Maybe she can see that there's still life and love out there for us.

For her.

We don't talk about my dad. Ever. After he died she took down the pictures, and that was that.

He was erased. I don't want it to be like that anymore. I want her to acknowledge that he existed. And maybe if she sees that it's okay for me to move on, she will too, and that will help her.

I just wish we didn't have to do this *today*. I wish we could have put it off a little longer. I'm going crazy climbing the walls of this place, waiting for him to get here, waiting for the judgment to begin.

My mom doesn't cook, so I've taken to throwing together a big pot of spaghetti, and I keep checking the noodles and tapping my fingers on the counter. I'm not even hungry and I've cooked the whole box.

This is a disaster in the making. I just know it. No matter how many ways I picture it going, it's never perfect.

I'm draining the noodles when I hear the rumble of his broken exhaust. It seems like he's punching the gas or something. It's roaring. I know my mom can see it from her bedroom window. I cringe. I wonder what she's doing, if she's looking down at that dilapidated truck as it pulls up to my cute little Mazda. I hope she doesn't judge him for that.

He rings the doorbell and I dump half the noodles in the sink, trying to get this done and get to the door before she does, but I don't make it in time.

The door is swinging open and she's at it.

"Mom, I got it," I say.

"Don't be silly. I want to meet him." She's really done up today, in a flowered sundress and big pearl earrings with a matching pearl necklace. She has bright lipstick and heels on.

Geez, she looks like she belongs at the Kentucky Derby.

"Hello! I'm Miranda," she says, holding out her hand, her fingers turned downwards. What does she expect? Is he supposed to kiss it or something?

"Connor. Nice to meet you." He shakes her hand but it's kind of turned down still, so it looks awkward, and I know he's noticed.

He's wearing a nice button-up today, with a clean pair of jeans. The shirt is a little wrinkled and his shoes are scuffed, but he looks good, and when he turns to smile at me, I see he's nervous. He's trying so hard. And he's so out of his element in this fancy foyer with the marble floors.

"Come on, I'll show you my room," I say, desperate to extract him from the situation. "And yes, I know, we'll leave the door open and all that."

I grab his hand and drag him past my mom. I'm sure she has a barrage of questions for him, but I'll let him see my room and I'll hug him and reassure him first, and then he'll be ready.

We take the stairs two by two, and in moments we're in my room, with its gauzy canopy bed and big bay window and perfectly matched white furniture. The carpet is thick and plush and clean and my clothes are hanging neatly in the closet, where I put them just an hour ago after picking them up off the floor.

I have a collection of pictures in a mishmash of different frames spread across my dresser, and a few scarves hanging on the edge of my four-poster bed, but otherwise everything is clean and clutter-free.

"Wow. This is nice," he says. "Totally you."

I sit on the edge of my bed and grin. "You like?"

He nods. "Yeah. It's great."

He walks over and sits next to me. "I knew your house was big and all, but it's even nicer than I realized. Your room makes mine look…" His voice trails off and he shrugs.

I laugh. "Oh, don't even think like that. I love your room. It's our home base. This is… this isn't cozy and comfortable like yours."

"You mean tiny and cramped."

I laugh again. I love how I feel when he's around. I love how untouchable I am, how I just can't stop grinning and laughing with him. "No. I mean, I love your room."

He leans over and kisses me, and it's a long, lingering kiss that reminds me of our almost-hook-up the weekend before.

But before anything can happen, I hear my mom clear her throat. She's standing in the doorway. "I'm ready for dinner when you are," she says.

I try to ignore the way my face burns at being caught red-handed. It's probably flaming red.

She leads the way down the hall and down the stairs, and then we gather around the big table in the formal dining room. We never eat in this room. It's too stuffy, even for her.

I guess it's kind of nice that she wanted this to be special, though. I guess it means she's going to try really hard to like him and make him feel welcome.

"So, Connor, where did you go to school? Here in Westport?"

I shove a big forkful of spaghetti in my mouth and grin at it. She's unknowingly stumbled upon the first of a barrage of topics that will make him uncomfortable.

"No. I have a GED."

"Oh. I see."

"I got it when I was sixteen," he adds.

"That's wonderful," she says. I wonder if she really thinks that. For me, she wants straight A's, honor society, Ivy League. Like what she had. Yet she's been so out of it since Dad died, I wonder if she's ever even noticed I'm not Ivy League material.

"And work? What do you do?"

Oh, God, she had to ask that.

"I'm, uh, I'm in between jobs right now."

"Oh." She turns a little pink. She knows she's putting her foot in her mouth now.

I hate the look on his face. The realization that he's unworthy in her eyes, even though she's trying to hide it. It's breaking my heart. He wants so much to be independent and good at things so he can prove his father was wrong about everything he ever said about him, and my mother is undoing it all without even trying.

"I got an A on my physics test," I say. The subject change is so obvious it's painful, but my mom looks grateful.

"That's great, honey."

"It's only the first one, but a lot of people flunked. Only one person got better than me."

Connor is looking at me differently right now. I hope he isn't thinking I'm trying to show him up. I can't interpret his stare.

"Wow. You're *really* smart," he says. "I mean, I knew you were, but that's awesome."

I smile and stare at my spaghetti. My mom has to see how supportive he is. This is good.

"Ann has always been brilliant," she says to him. "I knew it from the moment she was born. She's bound for greatness."

I can't believe how proud she sounds. I stare at her, wondering where all this is coming from. She's *bragging* about me. I mean, she used to do that all the time, but it's been a while. She's been wrapped up in … stuff.

"She learned to play the piano when she was eight,"

she says. "Her father and I wanted her to play the violin, but she hated the thing."

Connor smiles at me. "Sounds like her. She's rather stubborn."

"Tell me about it," my mom says.

And finally, all the tension is gone.

October 24

His father came back today. For good. There were bags scattered around the front door. That was how I knew.

He didn't come out of their bedroom when I walked past it. I was kind of glad. I don't think I want to meet him.

Now Connor and I are sitting on the hardwood floors in his room, debating whether or not he should introduce me. Neither of us can decide if I want to meet him.

I know so little of him. Just little pieces that tell me he's not a good guy. Pieces that say he's made Connor's life hell.

"Shit, let's just do this," he says. Connor is on edge, a little fidgety and uncomfortable looking, like the neck on his shirt is just too tight. He stands up grabs my hand and pulls me to my feet. I want to reach up and do something silly, like ruffle his adorable blond hair, but it seems stupid so I don't.

I've never even seen a picture of Jack. I don't know what he looks like. Nancy took them all down when Jack left three months ago.

Connor told me not to get used to it. He said his dad would be back.

He was right.

Connor knew exactly how it would work. For a few weeks, his mom would act as if it was out of the question. She wouldn't speak of Jack. It would be like he was dead.

But she would slowly lose her resolve. His name would be spoken again. Just in passing. Like, "Oh, Jack used to ..." or "Not that one, Jack broke it. Hand me the other one." But after that it would progress. She would say things like, "I wonder what he's doing right now."

Or "I think I might call him."

And when she hit that point, it would progress rapidly. Within a few weeks, Jack would be back. And Connor predicted it. Step by step, he knew what would happen.

For those weeks he was gone, it was bliss. Though I'm sure it was in the back of Connor's mind all the time, it was gone from mine. Jack existed only in stories. And he could not touch us.

And yet now I'm following Connor, my hand so small in his, through the cluttered house. And now we stand here at his parents' bedroom door, listening as the TV blares. Neither of us moves to knock on it; we just stand in silence. Finally he squeezes my hand, then lets it go and knocks.

I hear Nancy call us in, and we step inside their room.

Jack sits on the edge of the bed, a bag of Doritos in his lap and a beer can on the table beside him. He's wearing a ratty T-shirt and a pair of grease-stained carpenter jeans.

"Hey, uh, Dad. I just wanted you to meet Ann. My girlfriend."

I smile politely and nod at him.

"Hi." He smiles a little, I think. It creases his beady little eyes. I can't really tell for sure, because he has a thick beard that obscures most of his mouth. It's gray and wiry.

I guess I pictured him more in his prime. I guess I pictured dark hair and bulging muscles. He's still tall, of course. He has to be at least six feet tall. But the man before me is just a man.

"Okay...well..." Connor just grabs my hand and we leave the room and return to his.

"He seems..." And I don't know what to say. Because if I say anything nice, it lessens the things he's done to Connor. And if I say something mean, I'm making fun of his father.

"I know."

And that's all we say. Connor slides a beat-up Scrabble box out from under his bed and we open it up and start turning all the letters over.

"He's not bad when he's sober," he finally says.

"Oh." What am I supposed to say to that?

"He managed it for a few months when I was thirteen. We thought he was doing so well. But he started acting like an asshole again. And then I knocked over a trash can in the garage. The bottles and cans went everywhere. He hit me for that. For making a mess, he said. But I think it was because I told my mom he was drinking again."

He doesn't usually say things like this, so nonchalant. He just says little pieces of the truth, and I'm left trying to figure out the puzzle of his past. He hasn't opened up like this before.

I've never seen the whole hand of cards. He holds it close to his chest. But I'm glad he trusts me. We've been together less than two months, but it feels like we've never been apart.

Connor spells out HOUSE on the board.

I chew on my lip and stare at the letters on my little tray, trying to decide between REGRETS and GREEN.

"You look cute when you do that," he says.

I look up and smile at him and he smiles back, his eyes bright. I love these moments. These moments when he forgets about Jack because he's thinking of me.

I finally choose GREEN and mark down my points. My hair slides into my eyes as I scribble down the number, and before I can move it, he does it for me. His fingers slide the strands back behind my ear and he leaves his hand there, his fingers on the edge of my jaw and his thumb brushing my cheek, back and forth as he stares at me with his dark blue eyes.

We stay like that for longer than normal, just staring at one another.

And I know in that moment that I love him. I know in that moment that I am his, and that I don't want to be anywhere else but in this room right now, staring back at him.

"I love you," he says. It seems like he's been saying it since we met, though I guess it's only been a few weeks. Still, it's like he knew the moment we went on that first date that he'd fall in love with me, and he just had to wait for me to love him back. Maybe because no one else ever gives him a chance, and I did.

He's been speaking those three words while I smile and hug him and stay silent, and the desire to say it back grows.

"I love you too."

His eyes melt. He looks deeper at me, like he wants to see it in my eyes, like he wants to know it's true.

"You swear?" he says. It comes out like a whisper. We're still not moving, just staring and frozen like this.

"Yes. I swear. I love you."

He crawls across the Scrabble board and the words go everywhere, but neither of us care. He kisses me long and hard and I close my eyes, and I feel the urgency behind his lips.

In seconds I'm lying back against the ground, and the letters are tangling in my hair, and he's kissing me, his hands on my face, and there is a raw need that has never been there before. But I feel it too. I feel the heat, the absolute thirst for him.

I know his door isn't locked, but I know, too, that no one will bother us. They exist in Connor's world, but he doesn't exist in theirs.

His hands slide up my shirt. I pull on his, too, and in seconds we are naked from the waist up and he's kissing me everywhere. My arms, my shoulders, my chest, my stomach. Every inch of me, as if he can't get enough. Quick, butterfly kisses. His eyelashes tickle and set me on fire.

When he pulls my jeans off, I'm thankful it is dark, because I have never been unclothed like this in front of him. I have never let him see me like this.

As if he can read my thoughts, he pulls a blanket over us so that we are cloaked in it.

When he reaches into the nightstand, my heart nearly stops. I know what he's getting.

And I suddenly freeze. I think I'm ready for this. I am, right?

But as he pulls the little wrapper from the box, I'm paralyzed. The only thing moving is my chest, as it rises and falls with my panting.

And he knows, and he closes the drawer again.

"I'm … we can still …" I say.

"No," he whispers in my ear. He lies on top of me so that every inch is touching me, skin on skin. "You're not ready."

He shifts his weight and props himself up on an elbow.

"I love you. You might think you're ready, but you're not."

"I *am* ready. I'm just scared."

"Then we'll wait until you're not."

I nod my head and blink back the tears. I love that he knows me like this. I love that I didn't have to say anything for him to know. I pull him closer so that my face rests against his shoulder and I close my eyes. All I can feel is his body heat.

And it feels good. I know I only have forty-two minutes left with him before I have to leave. Before curfew.

But I will enjoy our forty-two minutes. And tomorrow there will be more.

And the day after that.

And we will spend every moment together.

Because that is what I want.

August 30
ONE YEAR

Sweetheart? Can you even hear me?"

Yes, I can hear him. He is all I can hear. His voice is raspy, desperate, begging. I want to block it out but even if I had earplugs or headphones, I'd still hear it.

"I'm sorry, baby. I'm so sorry."

I don't want him to be sorry. I'm *sick* of sorrys.

I wanted to be his life preserver, the thing that would keep him afloat. Instead, he became my anchor. And I'm tired of drowning.

How could I not see that it would never change? That it would always be this?

"I'm going to leave for a little bit, okay?"

I lift my head up and look at the door, then at the window. The storm is still raging on, both outside and inside.

"I'll just go dry off somewhere and let things cool down, okay?"

He keeps saying okay, over and over, as if he can say it enough and make it true.

It will never be true. Things have never been okay with us. Maybe if I'd paid attention, I would have seen that on our first few dates. Maybe I would have noticed his possessiveness; maybe I would have seen the way he wrapped around me, made me his entire world, his obsession.

Maybe I would have felt the weight he placed on my shoulders, one tiny stone at a time.

I listen as his heavy footfalls leave me. The broken exhaust in his truck backfires as he starts it up, and then the rumble slowly disappears.

I lie back again and stare up at the ceiling. I close my eyes and will the sleep to come. Sleep is the only time when I feel at peace.

But when I sleep, I dream.

October 18

ONE MONTH, EIGHTEEN DAYS

Today is our first away meet for cross country. I'm a ball of nerves and excitement.

I won my first race two weeks ago. But winning at home is different. You know the terrain; you know when to kick it up a notch and when to coast. You know where the turns are and where to position yourself to keep the most momentum going.

At Reilly Hills, it's different. I've been here twice, but the last few hills still manage to surprise me. I always get passed at the last minute because I don't gauge it quite right and have nothing left.

But now I've trained harder than ever before, and I

can't wait to be the one who breaks the tape. I can't wait to feel the energy and the cheers as I win.

Blake and I sit next to each other on the bus, like we're supposed to since we're captains. It's a tradition or something. Coach thinks it gives the team confidence, like we're strategizing.

We're not talking, though. Ever since that awkward ... *moment* a few weeks ago, we haven't said much, and it's starting to get to me. We lead the team in our silent way. If one of us announces something, a warm-up or a stretch, the other just follows without a word.

Even though we've never been best friends, we've always been close. We have this sort of mutual respect for each other that comes from years of proving ourselves. I know Blake worked his butt off to get to this point. To be the best. I see him, all summer long, jogging the long back roads around town. He knows a real runner never has an off-season. And so each fall, it's like a reunion, and we hug and talk and catch up, and every year we get closer.

It's a forty-minute ride to Reilly Hills. It's going to be torture if we don't speak, and I hate that we've been reduced to this. I can't tolerate the prickly feeling every time we hit a bump and my shoulder rubs his. I can't tolerate the way he's staring out the window, as if he doesn't even know I'm there.

So I break the silence myself. "So, um, do you hate me now or what?"

He turns and gives me this look, like he's shocked I

finally talked. "No. *God.* I don't hate you. I just thought...I figured I made you uncomfortable or something."

"Oh, no, it's not that. I just didn't know what to say, after...you know."

And then there's silence again, and I worry that it's back for good.

"*Okay*, well now that that's over," he says, and laughs.

And Blake is back.

"Congrats on winning last week, by the way," he adds.

"You too. Two in a row. Well done."

He grins at me, in that way of his. The way that says *I know I'm good* without being cocky. I don't know how he does it, but he has this comfortable, confident air about him.

"So, this boyfriend of yours," he says.

I nod my head, a little worried about what he's going to say next. "Yeah?"

He grins at me. "If he hurts you, I swear to God I'll knock him out."

I smack his leg with the back of my hand. "Oh, quit it, he's a good guy."

"He must be. He's got good taste in girls."

I smile in relief. Obviously Blake isn't so embarrassed about the... *event* in the woods. That's good. Maybe we can stay friends. Three years is too much to give up on so easily.

"In another life, we would have been perfect, you know."

I look at him out of the corner of my eye and try not to smile. "Shut up," I say, the smile finally taking over as I playfully swipe at him again.

He raises his hands in mock-surrender. "I'm just sayin'."

I slide down a bit on the bench and prop my knees up on the seat in front of us. "Maybe. Guess we'll never know."

He slides down so we're shoulder to shoulder again. "Okay, but do you have any hot friends?"

"Blake!"

"What? You can't blame me for trying," he says. He shoots me another of his cocky grins, and it makes my cheeks warm.

"You're impossible." I raise an eyebrow, try to act like I'm not finding him even a *little* attractive, but I'm not sure it works. There's no denying that Blake is good looking.

"That's what they tell me."

I shake my head again, but the grin is there to stay. I'm glad Blake is who he is. It makes all this so much easier.

He drums his fingers on the seat between us, though there's hardly any free space, and his fingers keep brushing my thigh. My warm-ups are so thin I can feel the heat on my leg. "How 'bout whoever runs the fastest time overall leads calisthenics next week?"

"Plus walk-out duty."

"Deal." His fingers stop their drumming and he reaches out to grasp my hand.

And then we shake on it, and I know I'm doomed. Blake will win. But the knowing smile on his face right now makes it all worth it.

October 9

ONE MONTH, NINE DAYS

Connor and I are at a park, a few blocks from the ocean, acting like kids. It's a beautiful sunny day, with a slight salty breeze that cools our skin. He pushes me on the swings, and I laugh and stare at the sky and wonder what it would be like to just let go and fly into the air, and land in a heap in the gravel.

I wonder if it would hurt.

I bet it would, but I bet for those moments I would be free as a bird, and it would be glorious.

Connor sits on a swing next to me and pumps his legs, picking up speed and height, and before I know it we're paralleling each other, my hair wild around my face.

It's weird. Whenever we get to the top, there's this moment that seems to freeze, and all I can see is his face, and the sky, and nothing else. But then it is broken and we're swinging downwards again, only to repeat it on the other side, dozens of frozen moments strung together.

Eventually I get dizzy and drag my feet, and he does the same, and we stop. I twist my swing a few times, absently turning around and then back again, my legs sticking straight out in front of me.

Whenever he's around, everything feels charged. I'm filled with energy, and I want to go wild with it and scream and dance and kiss.

But all I have to do is stare into his intense blue eyes, and it calms me, and I just want to be close to him.

I look at his hand where it grips the chain of the swing. Scars. They cover his knuckles, white lines that crisscross all over his fist.

He sees me looking, and he drops his hand and looks at it, too. "I have a temper problem," he says. "Sometimes I have to hit something. But I'm not like my dad. I just hit *things*, not people. I got these when I punched out a window in the garage."

"Oh." I don't know what to say. His dad hits people? And does that mean that Connor's been one of them? The thought makes me a little bit sick. I'm not sure I understand an anger like that, an anger so fierce you could hurt someone.

"I know it sounds bad. I haven't done anything like

that in a long time, though. These were when I was thirteen. Things were just so rough back then."

"Oh," I say again. I sound so stupid. I have no idea what I'm supposed to say, what the appropriate response is in a conversation like this. The things he's talking about are so different than the things I'm used to.

He grabs the chain on my swing and I look at him and meet his intense stare. "I swear to you, I would never hurt you. Never."

I nod my head. I see the conviction in his face. I hear it in his voice. I know he would never hurt me.

I know his word is good. And I trust him.

And I know he trusts me, because he's telling me his secrets. He's telling me his hurt. And I know I can do the same. I know I could tell him anything. And because of what he's been through, because of what he's lived, he won't judge me for it.

Even though Abby is my best friend, she lives this amazing charmed life and I've never wanted to tell her the bad parts of mine. I've never wanted to tell her how sometimes I lie awake at night and the house is big and empty and I can hear my mom crying herself to sleep, and it scares me and I want to go hug her but I know she doesn't want me to know she does it. And so I lie in the dark and listen to the sounds, and each one tears at me until sometimes it makes me cry, too.

And yet I don't say anything to my mom and she goes on doing what she does, and I go on pretending I don't know.

It feels wrong, though. I think I should tell her I know, and I should be there for her, but I need her as much as she needs me, and so we just stay this way forever, a stalemate of tears. And Abby has no idea.

But now I have Connor. And I know he'll understand me.

And I'm ready to tell him everything.

October 8

ONE MONTH, EIGHT DAYS

'm in bed when he calls. I know it is him, because no one else calls me this late.

I pick it up before the first ring is over, my heart thundering in my chest from waking up so abruptly.

"Hello?"

"Ann?"

His voice is so small.

"Yeah. It's me."

I'm wide awake now. I roll over and prop my head up on the pillows, the receiver gripped hard in my hand.

"I—" He stops.

"Is something wrong?" He sounds so different. Something's up. He's calling even later than usual and he sounds so small.

"I just ... No. Nothing."

"Tell me."

"I'm alone. And I'm just in a ... funny mood. I'm sorry. I shouldn't have called so late."

"No. Please it's okay. Just talk to me. I'm awake now."

I stifle a yawn.

"I miss you," he says. And it sounds cute. I can picture the way his lips are curling upward as he says it. "What are you wearing?"

I giggle.

"Oh, I love that sound," he says. "You've just made my night."

I smile, as if he will see it.

"But seriously, what are you wearing?"

"I'm not telling you that!"

"Come on, please?"

There's that voice again. That cute, flirty, appealing voice that makes me grin every time.

"Okay. A yellow tank top and plaid boxers that are at least two sizes too big. Sexy, right?" I laugh.

"Oh, that sounds hot." And then he laughs. "God, this is crazy. Two minutes of talking to you and you've completely changed my mood. I wish you could be here right now."

"Me too."

"You should come over."

"It's midnight!"

"So?"

"So, there's no way I can get out of here without my mom knowing it."

He sighs. "I know. But I'm glad you answered. I'd been bumming and stressing out about stuff, and I just needed someone to talk to."

"You can call anytime. I love talking to you," I say. Is it stupid to be grinning like this? How can he make me feel this way?

"We should do something fun tomorrow."

"I have school. And cross country."

"So? Skip."

Is it wrong that I'm tempted? More tempted than I've ever been? I'm seventeen, and I've never played hooky before. Not without Mom's permission, anyway, and that hardly counts.

"I don't know..."

"Come on. I can't sleep, so I'll plan a whole day for us. I'll surprise you."

God, I love surprises too. Especially his. They're always the best.

"Just this once, though," I say.

"Yes. Once."

"Okay. Fine. Deal. Abby will cover for me."

I can practically *hear* his smile.

"Awesome. Okay, I'm going to hang up and plan this."

"All right."

"Thank you. For answering. For being you. For making me feel so good."

I know he means it because his voice is different. It went from lonely to happy, and I love that I did that for him.

"Anytime."

"'Night. Sweet dreams."

"You too," I say.

And then I hang up, a smile on my face.

September 30

ONE MONTH

I'm at Connor's house. Lately, our dates are stretching out, getting longer and longer and progressively closer to my supposed curfew. He takes me to dinners and movies and walks and everywhere he can think of, but we always end up back here, unwilling to let it end until we have to.

I know my mom won't catch me if I stay late once in a while. But I'm afraid if I start pushing it, I'll never stop, and before I know it I'll just never leave his side.

His presence is incredibly … addicting. When I'm around him, I can't stop smiling and laughing and staring at him, and he's the same way with me, and sometimes we can spend hours just staring at each other. Sometimes I think the clock is actually ticking in my ear, it's so loud. I can never stop thinking about how fast it moves when I'm with him and how the end of it is always barreling toward me.

And it seems totally crazy that everything is happening like this, so fast. Just a month ago I didn't know him, and now he's infiltrating everything and he's all I think about when we're apart.

And so every day I wait for night, when I will be here, with him. Today we're playing Jenga, trying to get the tower taller than our record twenty-six layers. He has a pile of board games in his closet, crammed between basketballs, car magazines, cookbooks... all his hobbies. I'm amazed by them, how he knows so much about so many things. It's my turn, and I keep cheating, sliding a block a little bit and then changing my mind and putting it back, and it's become a joke. I get one halfway out before the tower starts to lean, and then I push it back and watch the whole thing wobble, a wicked grin on my face as he watches me more than the tower. It's intense, sometimes, that feeling of his eyes on me. I'm the only thing in the world to him. We can be in a store or a restaurant or anywhere, and he always watches me over anything else.

This is so much fun. Every moment of it.

I think I have it made as I easily slide a piece out—my sixth choice—but as I pick it up I manage to hook the edge of the tower and the whole thing topples, and I laugh and throw the pieces into the air.

"Gah! I suck at this," I say, and then lie back on the

ground and toss my remaining piece in the air, the one I'd so carefully selected.

He leans over, his face just inches from mine. "I try so hard to let you beat me, but I still keep winning." His breath is warm on my face and smells minty, like he brushed his teeth right before I came over. And then he kisses me and I forget all about the game and the blocks crammed underneath my back and legs, and I lose myself in it.

When it's over, and he pulls away just a few inches, I grin at him and he smiles back.

"Where've you been all my life?" he says, finally sitting upright again.

"Waiting for you," I say, only half joking. I toss a Jenga block at him and it bounces off his shoulder.

He shakes his head. "This just seems too perfect to be real. *You* are too perfect."

I shake my head. "No. I'm really not. You just haven't known me long enough to see my flaws. I assure you, they're plentiful."

I'm still half joking, and he laughs and kisses me again. "I don't care. I love you."

The room goes dead silent, and his eyes widen just the tiniest bit, like he realizes too late what he'd just said aloud.

Three words I haven't heard in years, not from anyone, not even my mom. Three tiny little words that make me feel so big. He can't mean it. I rush to fix it. "It's okay, I mean, I can just pretend like you didn't—"

"No," he says. "No, don't pretend like I didn't say it. I mean it. I do love you. And it's okay that you don't say it yet because I know it's been so fast, and it's okay if you don't feel it yet, but I want you to know, I love you."

I swallow and nod my head, wondering if I'm ready for this, wondering if I can handle him being in love with me.

But I'm also wondering if I'm already in love with him. Because these things I feel, they're so strong, so overwhelming, and there's times I can't stand to be away from him. Times I have to leave because it's 10:50 and I'm about to miss curfew, and yet I don't want to leave, and my goody-goody side wars with my absolute desire to throw every last rule away and just *stay* and hope my mom doesn't even notice.

He kisses me again and we lean back against his bed, our fingers intertwined. I see our reflection in the mirror across from us, and I wonder: is it too soon to be thinking *forever*?

September 20

Abby and I are lounging on her bed, staring at the ceiling through the gauze of her canopy bed. A bag of Doritos and a tub of gourmet chocolates sit between us, and empty cans of Diet Coke adorn the nightstands. We're supposed to be working on our new, year-long English project, but neither of us can muster the motivation.

"I don't see why we have to choose a classic," she says. "We should be able to pick any book, really. What's so great about Shakespeare and Chaucer and Salinger?"

I chew on my lip. "I don't know. I'd rather read *The Vampire Diaries*."

"I'd rather watch *The Vampire Diaries*," Abby says.

I snort. "I doubt listing the reasons a vampire makes a good boyfriend will get us anywhere."

Abby sighs. "Let's just go with Shakespeare. We have to read and contrast at least three works, right? And at least there are CliffsNotes and movie versions."

I twist a purple knit scarf around my hand as I consider this. "I guess."

"Good. Now we can go do something else," she says, and then reaches into the Doritos bag.

"I've been dying to get to the craft store in town. I have this idea of something to do for Connor."

We finally sit up, something we haven't done for nearly an hour. The sugar rushes to my head and I have to sit still for a moment until it clears.

"That's totally sweet. When do I get to meet him, anyway?" She's already pulling on her shoes, which I take to mean she's down with the craft store trip.

I slide my arms into a zip-up hoodie. "Soon. Maybe next weekend or something. He hasn't met my mom or anything either. It's kind of new still."

"Oh, please, you're head over heels," she says as she switches off her bedroom light and we walk toward the front entry.

"Well, sort of," I say, suddenly feeling shy about the whole topic. I've never done the boyfriend thing before.

I follow Abby to her car and slide into one of the leather bucket seats.

"Well, you guys have kissed, right?"

I grin sheepishly.

"Oh, my God, you have. Why didn't you tell me? I totally would have told you!"

I shrug.

"It's a long ride to the store. Spill. Now."

"Where do I start?"

———

Twenty minutes later, we're strolling the aisles at the craft store looking for some special glue required for glass. Abby decides she needs her own craft so that we can work on them together, and she's currently grabbing stickers for a scrapbook.

"What about this?" I say, showing her some sheets of beach balls and pails and little sand castles.

"Sure. Sounds good!"

I nod and toss a few sheets into the basket. It is filling up quickly, as if Abby intends to document every day of her life.

"I think we probably have enough. Let's go to the beach and find some sea glass. Then we can both get started."

Abby nods and reluctantly leaves the spinning display of stickers behind as we head to the cashiers.

I link my elbow with hers. "What page are you doing first?"

She smiles. "Well, I have this really annoying friend,

see. So I was thinking I'd put together a few pages and draw little horns all over her and black out her eyes."

I snicker.

Sixty-two dollars later, we leave the store, our hands filled with bags of supplies.

I wonder what Connor will think when I hand him my heart.

September 19

TWO WEEKS, SIX DAYS

I'm sitting on a stool at our kitchen counter, swinging my legs and slurping at the milk at the bottom of my cereal bowl. There are cartoons on in the background, even though I'm too old for them. I don't really watch them anymore, but it wouldn't be Saturday if they weren't on.

My mom is up. I can hear the water running. Sometimes her showers last forty-five minutes, and I have no idea what she does during that time, but when she emerges she never looks fresh and relaxed; her eyes are puffy and she looks like the walking dead.

I don't really know what she does at any time, really. We're strangers in the same house. I want it to be different.

I want to hug her and say *I love you*. But I don't think she'll magically hug me and smile and say *I love you too*, and that's what she does in my mind when I say it to her, and I'd rather have that than reality.

My dad would be so disappointed if he knew what had happened to "his girls." He tried to so hard to be the glue for so many years, so many rounds of chemo, so many everything. Even as my mom took on that haunted look toward the end and even as I cried myself to sleep those last couple months, he couldn't change the facts, and then one day it was done and he was gone.

I try to remember my mom before he died. Those days before she died with him. I try to remember the times she'd declare it was girls' day and no dads were allowed, and I'd grin at him when she said it, and we'd get our nails done and go shopping and eat six-dollar fruit smoothies.

She was a good mom. She was everything I ever needed or wanted. And cruel reality stole her from me, and she became something else, and I became no one to her, because she can't see through her own tears long enough to realize how much it hurts me.

I know if it had been reversed, Dad wouldn't do this. Even when he was really dying he stayed strong and was there for me. Even when he was sick he would sit in a lawn chair, all wrapped up in a blanket, shivering against the cold just so he could hang out at the park with me. And my mom was next to him, every single time. We were a real family then.

I wish one day I would look up and she would be standing there at the finish line of a race, beaming at me. I wish she would stop wallowing long enough to be proud of me, long enough to see that I'm growing and becoming someone, something. But she never will.

She doesn't really even have friends anymore. They just drifted away like sand on the wind, and it became just us. And now it is just her.

Eventually her shower turns off and after several long moments of silence, I hear her walking across the ceiling, down the hall, and down the steps. Her footsteps are soft and quiet, like a mouse.

I finish the last drop of Fruity Pebbles–flavored milk and turn to see her.

Her blond hair is still damp and tangled, but her mask of makeup is on and she's wearing a cute button-up blouse with khaki pants. Even on weekends she looks like a lawyer. I think that's all she wants to be. Just a *thing* and not a person.

She sits down next to me and grabs the cereal box, and I twist around and watch the cartoons from my seat at the counter, and for a long time we just sit there and I listen to her eat and try to concentrate on the cartoon dog on the screen.

"Sleep okay?" she asks.

I don't know why that's her favorite question. Maybe because I think she doesn't sleep at all. Maybe it's her veiled way of asking if I'm okay.

"Yep. You?"

"Uh-huh."

I want to tell her it's a lie, that she would look rested if she slept at all, but I don't.

And I decide I can't do this same song and dance today. So I just blurt out, "Do you want to … I don't know, do something today?"

She stops chewing even though her mouth is full and looks over at me. "I have a lot of new cases to review. Some other time?"

Some other time. It's always some other time. I want to know when that other time is, but maybe if I knew, I'd never ask again.

"Yeah. Sure."

And then I slide off my stool and go upstairs to change into jeans and a tank top, and I will leave and be gone all day, because that is what I do.

And today will just be another day in a long chain of disappointments, but that is how it is now.

That's just how it works.

September 14

TWO WEEKS, ONE DAY

Cross country starts today. It is my fall sport. It signals that school has begun, that the leaves will soon drop, and that my schedule will be full again.

Blake and I will be captains this year, him of the boys, me of the girls. He's better than I am, but I'm the only senior girl on the team this year, so I win by default.

We jog side by side through the outdoor halls and courtyards of the school, toward the woods and trails behind the football field. There are twenty-seven runners behind us, their footfalls sounding out a rhythm that pushes me forward with each beat. We keep an easy pace, talking all the while. Those who fall back will be cut. If

Blake and I can talk and they can't even run, they are not cut out for this.

It doesn't take long for us to hit our stride. We have been on this team for three years together. We have worn down these paths with our own feet, first as gangly, slow freshmen, and now as the veterans who hold the team together. Today, the sun is shining in its full glory, a last day of summer weather before fall defeats it.

"I got Bellnik for history," Blake says as we enter the woods and the shade of trees.

"Ouch." My feet are making pleasant little crunching noises now as they fall upon the first leaves of autumn. I know I should hate that an entire school year stretches out before me, but on days like this, I just revel in it. In the promise of a new year and new sports and crisp weather and winter holidays.

"I know. And I got Miss Valentine for pre-cal."

"Double-ouch," I say. My breathing is steady. My muscles are warm. I'm happy and comfortable and ready for a long run.

Blake glances back at the runners behind us. Some of them are already thinning out, and we've only gone two miles. "There will definitely be some cuts next week."

I nod and look over at him. His cheeks are flushed with the blood pumping through him and his dark hair has lost its perfectly gelled look. It's a mess, thanks to the wind and the branches we duck under.

Sometime over the summer, he grew up. He doesn't look like the kid from junior year, arms and legs too long and scrawny for his body. Now he looks fit, and healthy, and *good*.

And as he looks back at me I can't help but wonder what he's thinking. Have I changed?

"You keeping up okay?" he says.

I grin. "Absolutely. I could sprint the next two miles."

"Is that a challenge?" he asks, returning my smile. His Adidas track pants are swish-swish-swishing with each stride.

I glance back at the rest of the team, wondering if they can handle picking up the pace.

Half of them can. And that's enough. "Yes."

And then I take off. I crank it up a notch and my legs are flying now, leaping over twisted tree roots and splashing through puddles, and I can hear Blake's thundering steps behind me, and it pushes me harder, faster, until the forest streams by in a blur of brown and green. Everything disappears, and all I can hear is my breathing and my heartbeat in my ears, and it is just me and the run.

When the trail forks, I take the left path, the longer one, knowing it's not part of the plans but unwilling to turn back toward school. I can still hear him behind me. He's keeping pace.

But he's not passing me.

We run on and on, until we are miles into the woods and I know we have to stop. My throat is turning sore with the cool air and my legs are beginning to feel the push.

And when we stop, and I finally see him, his face is reddened with exertion and his T-shirt is damp, but he's grinning a smile as wide as my own. "We lost them all. I'm betting they took the right turn. The turn we'd planned on. Rick probably took them that way after we lost them."

I grin sheepishly. "Can't say I blame 'em. We must be three miles from school if we cut through the trees. Four if we follow the path."

I lean against a tree, one foot propped up on it as I regain my breath. My chest is rising and falling, expanding as large as it will go as I rake in more oxygen.

"I say we follow the path. How long are we going to have weather like this? We can walk back. It won't take more than an hour or so."

I look up at the sky through the canopy. It's a vibrant blue. It must be barely four thirty. Plenty of time for a long walk, and it might end up being the last one of the season.

When I look down again, he's closer. Standing in front of me, inches away. He's still breathing a little hard. His eyes are looking straight at me, intense.

"What are you—"

And then he kisses me. It's salty, the taste of his mouth mingling with his sweat, and he still breathes heavily through his nose. I'm so stunned I don't move. For just a second, I actually *want* this, until finally I come back to focus and turn my head away, and our lips part.

For one millisecond, I regret it. For just a moment I think I might turn back to him and throw all my good sense away and kiss him.

But then I think of Connor, and I know I can't do that. "I...uh, I'm kind of seeing someone."

Suddenly I'm breathing hard again. Why does it feel so wrong and so right at the same time? Why couldn't we have done this last spring? Why didn't Blake just call me, or stop by Subway this summer? I'd even told him I could give him a free sandwich, knowing I'd have to pay for it after he left. But he never stopped by.

He turns around, so his back is to me, and I don't know what he's thinking. He just stands there, one hand cocked on his hip, staring down at a nearby stump. Why isn't he looking at me? "Who?"

"You don't know him. He doesn't go here. It's only been a couple weeks, but it's getting serious pretty fast."

"Oh."

And we just stand there like that, me staring at his back. "Blake, I'm sorry. Any other time—"

"We should get back. It looks like rain." His voice is curt. He doesn't want a conversation. He doesn't want my explanation, he just wants this over.

It's a lie. There's no way it's going to rain. But I don't correct him. I just stare at his back for another long, silent moment, trying to find someway to make sure what happened didn't just ruin our friendship, and yet I know there are no words that can fix this or make it so that it never happened. So I just follow him back down the path.

"Okay. Sure."

And for more than an hour, we don't talk.

September 12
ONE WEEK, SIX DAYS

After our third date, we go back to Connor's house. For some absurd reason, I feel nervous. I know his parents might be home. I've never "met the parents" before. Does this mean our relationship is real? That he's officially my boyfriend? Or does this just mean we're hanging out some more?

His house is cute. The lawn is perfectly mowed in diagonal stripes leading up to a red front door. There's a picket fence and everything. It's like the house you'd picture if you thought of the perfect family place, the American Dream.

He smiles at me as I walk up next to him on the sidewalk, and he slips his hand into mine. I love how comfortable we've gotten already. I love how he just holds my hand or slings his arm around my shoulder and kisses me on the cheek. I've never had more than a date or two before. I've never had someone just want to be close to me and I've never been comfortable like this.

We walk up the drive like that, hand in hand, and he pushes open the door.

"Mom?"

The house is quiet. There's no one home.

"Guess she's not here. Want to see my room?"

I nod. I could follow him anywhere.

He leads me through the living room and we turn at the hallway, and then we're walking through a white-paneled door and we're in his room. It has hardwood floors and sliding mirrored doors, and a big bed that seems to take up the entire room, and I'm trying hard to pretend I don't notice it. Why does this feel so weird? Why am I drawn to it right now?

I roll my eyes, careful to be sure Connor doesn't see my thoughts written all over my face.

"This is great," I say. The room is small and bare, like he's never taken the time to put posters or pictures up.

"Thanks. I know it's not much, but it's mine."

He sits down on the edge of his bed and lies back, staring at the ceiling. I stand there awkwardly until he pats the spot next to him, so I sit on the edge like he did and lie back.

This is surreal. I'm lying on a bed next to him. Fully clothed, my feet still on the ground, but still, sort of crazy.

"Sorry my mom's not here."

"It's okay. No biggie. Where's your … dad?"

God, why did I just ask that? I know his dad is an alcoholic! Why did I just ask that?

"He's been gone a few weeks. They're kind of separated right now."

"Oh. I'm sorry."

"I'm not."

His abrupt statement jars me. The room feels heavy.

"He's kind of a jerk, and whenever he's gone, life is just … so much better. But it won't last. He'll be back once he weasels his way back in. For now, though, it's all good."

"Oh."

"*Anyway*," he says, laughing. I laugh too. I'm glad he's got a sense of humor. "Want a milkshake?"

I grin. "I think that's the best thing I've heard all day."

And so we spend the rest of the afternoon gorging ourselves on ice cream and waiting for his mom to come home, but she never does. I leave just before curfew, and he is alone when I leave him.

September 6
SEVEN DAYS

Today is our second date. It's only been three days since our first one, but we couldn't wait any longer. I can't get him out of my head. I can't stop thinking of that cute smile, of the way it felt when he told me I'm beautiful, or the way his eyes lit up when I opened the front door and he saw me.

Today we're bowling. I'm a terrible bowler, and by the ninth frame I have a whopping thirty-two points. But we just keep laughing every time I hit a gutter ball, and I can't wipe the grin off my face no matter how many times I miss the pins.

Connor is good. He left out bowling on his list of hobbies. He played in a kid's league once, I guess. He probably won it all, if he was this good. He's two points shy of two hundred and he just got a strike, so I'm guessing he's going to top that.

I bowl two more gutter balls and then switch back into my street shoes while I watch him get another strike, his arm rolling the ball straight down the middle as if it's effortless. When it's all over, he has a two-forty. Amazing. Is he this good at everything?

I wait for him while he takes off those red and white shoes and switches back into a pair of Vans. He's wearing this dark V-neck sleeveless thing, like a sweater vest or something, and it looks kind of silly on him. I've known him less than a week and I can tell it's not his style. But I also kind of think it's cute, because I'm pretty sure he put it on for me.

I think he saw my house and got all intimidated or something, because his outfit has *trying too hard* written all over it, in the most adorable way. And I want to tell him not to worry about impressing me, but I know that means pointing out that his outfit is all wrong, so I'm not going to do it. I just keep smiling to myself when he's not looking, and think about him trying on a dozen different shirts.

He holds the door open for me and when we walk across the lot to his truck, he slips his hand into mine. I smile at him when he does it, and try not to let my heart leap when he gives my hand a little squeeze. I have that nervous energy around him again, that adrenaline-charged heart. I don't know how he can have this effect on me, but he does. Seven days after meeting him and I can't stop obsessing over every smile and look and laugh.

He opens the truck door for me and I slide in. Once he's inside, I look over at him and smile, and then it happens. He leans over to me, and before I know what I'm doing, I close my eyes and his lips are on mine, soft, and we're kissing.

We're kissing.

I forget to breathe. When he pulls away, I let out a long sigh and then take a big ragged breath to fill my lungs.

"Sorry. I didn't want to wait and have that awkward front door thing."

I grin at him.

"Fine with me. But I still want another at the front door."

He grins back at me and fires up the truck. "I think I can handle that."

I think I can too.

"Did you have fun tonight?" he asks.

I chew on my lip to keep the grin from spreading from ear to ear, the grin that gives me away as a silly lovesick girl after only two dates. "Yes. Tons."

"So do you … do you want to do it again sometime?"

I turn to look at him, and he's staring at the road as if it takes every last ounce of concentration and he can't tear his eyes away to look at me, but I know his heart is probably beating out of control like mine is.

"Yes. Definitely."

And then his lips curl into a smile and he looks over at me. "Sounds good."

And when we get to my house, he walks me to the door and we kiss a few more times, and all I can think of is our next date, when we can do it all again.

For the first time, someone is seeing me, and I want to catch up from a thousand days of being invisible.

September 3
FOUR DAYS

Today I'm going out with Connor. I can't believe it. He actually called after I gave him my number. I fully expected to be blown off. Guys just don't ask me out like this. I'm not outgoing enough to be noticed.

And now I'm a ball of nerves, practically bouncing off the walls. I've been on, like, four dates in my whole life, and two of them were homecoming dances where I went with someone "as friends" even though I wanted it to be more.

And I don't even know where we're going. It's a surprise. I tried to get it out of him, but he held fast, and I have no idea what we're doing tonight, if it's going to be dinner and a movie or something totally different.

I kind of like that. School starts in two days, and when all I can think of is our date, it makes it seem so far away.

Connor said to dress casual, so I wear a cute pair of jeans, low heels, and two layers of tank tops, one baby blue and one yellow. My hair is swept up in a messy bun and I wear dangly little earrings. Stars. I hope I look okay. I hope he doesn't take one look at me and change his mind and decide he was totally crazy for asking me out.

He pulls up in a beat-up Ford F-150, the one he was driving the day I met him. I can see him from my window. It rumbles at the curb for a minute until he kills it and climbs out, and I can hear the door squeak. I want to watch him but I don't want to keep him standing on the porch, so I don't. I grab my bag and take the stairs two by two, and swing open the door just as he makes it up the last step.

He looks amazing. He has on dark jeans and a blue T-shirt and the biggest smile I've ever seen. It lights up his eyes. His hands are behind his back, and when he holds them out I see what they contain: daisies and baby's breath. Yellow and white, the perfect summer mix.

Warmth spreads through me and I have to fight not to drop my jaw, I'm so surprised and pleased by his gesture. Instead I just grin, and I hope it's half as amazing as the smile on Connor's face right now. "Thank you!"

Before I know what I'm doing I stand on my tippy toes and kiss him on the cheek, and then we both turn a little red. I have no idea why I was that forward.

"Let me toss these in water and then we can go."

Too late, I realize I should have invited him in, because he just stands there on the porch while I rush off to the kitchen and drop the bouquet in a vase. But it only takes me seconds and I'm back in no time.

He walks to the truck and holds the door open for me, and I slide over the cracked vinyl seats as his cologne washes over me. I breathe deeply, enjoying the scent. Before I'm buckled he's around to his side and jumping in and firing up the truck. It's even louder inside, but he doesn't seem to notice. He just puts it in gear and before I know it, we're winding down Snob Hill, our windows rolled down and the salty ocean air whipping through the cab.

"Where are we going?" I ask.

He just shakes his head and smiles, this cute half-smile that lifts the edges of his full lips. Why am I staring at his lips? "Still not telling."

I roll my eyes and smirk a little, enjoying the playful way he says it, but I don't ask again. I kind of like that he hasn't told me yet. Everyone always gives in and tells their secrets.

He turns right at the bottom of the hill, away from town and the beach, and now I'm really curious. He takes a few turns, winds back up toward the mountains and then down a gravel road, then parks on the edge of the pavement. "Come on. It's a short hike."

I nod and slide out of the truck, realizing that heels, even low ones, do not count as casual wear. Now I look totally out of place.

We don't walk far before I start having trouble. Late

summer rains have made the ground moist and my heels are sinking, and I'm walking with my arms out for balance like some crazy lunatic, my hands waving whenever one heel sinks further than the other. This is definitely not scoring me any points.

"How 'bout you put this backpack on and I'll give you a piggy back ride?"

My face heats up a little at the idea of jumping on his back. I've known him for all of three days. But if I want to know what his secret is, I need help. "Okay."

He kneels down and uses a tree trunk to keep his balance, and then he stands with my arms looped around his neck and my legs wrapped around his waist, and then we're walking again, much faster than before. "God, you weigh like two pounds," he says.

My face burns now. This is both awkward and really, really nice, and I can smell his cologne again, masculine and musky, and I have to fight the urge to rest my face against his back. His shoulders seem even broader, more heavily muscled, from this angle.

He weaves his way through the woods, stepping carefully over rocks and tree roots, and we end up at his destination in a few short minutes. Something is roaring. Loud.

"It's a waterfall," he says as I slide off his back. "We just have to get to that landing right there. There's steps built in. Planks. You should be able to get down without a problem, just grab that rope for balance."

I follow his directions and make it, wobbling on my heels all the while, down to a landing about fifteen feet below the trail we'd walked in on. There are a few fallen logs gathered around a big round chunk of tree, like a table and benches made by nature.

Connor unzips his backpack and reveals his secret: a picnic. He spreads out a tablecloth on the big round stump and starts laying out sandwiches and chips and a big thermos and some napkins. "There wasn't much at the house to choose from, so it's just some turkey sandwiches and lemonade…"

"It's perfect," I say. "Thank you."

This is the best date ever. It hasn't even started and it's the best date ever. Dinner and a movie? Forget that. I'd rather have a picnic and a waterfall.

I take a seat on one of the logs and watch as he arranges it all and hands me a paper plate, and then he sits down across from me, a plate in his own hands.

I can tell he's a little nervous, and it's cute. His face has the slightest red tinge and he keeps messing with his spiky blond hair and twisting his watch around his wrist in between bites.

"So… what kinds of things are you into?" I ask, after it seems like we've sat here too long without talking.

"Basketball, guitars, skateboarding, cooking—even though I'm horrible at it—working on cars—especially the classics—baseball cards, state quarters, sailboats, fishing, concerts, and movies, I guess."

"Wow," I say, laughing. "That's a lot of hobbies."

He nods. "Yeah, I guess so. I like to stay busy… and I get interested in a lot of different things, so I figure, why not? I hate when people talk about things and don't go out and do it, you know?"

"Yeah, I guess so. I mean, I'm just into running. I could spend every moment running if it wouldn't totally kill me. I do cross country and track."

"That's cool," he says. "I did basketball for a while. It's nice having people who just *get* why you're so into something."

"Exactly."

The silence stretches on for a few moments, and I want to fill it. "Any brothers or sisters?"

He shakes his head. "No. Just me. Thank God."

I laugh, but then I see he's serious. "Why thank God?"

He shrugs. "My dad's just ... my dad's an alcoholic," he says. So simply. So concise. And yet I see that those words were hard to spit out.

"Oh."

He half-heartedly shrugs. "I don't know why I just told you that. That's not really ... that's not really first-date material. So ... let's change the subject."

The waterfall still hums, sending gentle mist of river water over us. It feels ... ethereal? I'm not sure what it is, but this date feels like a dream, like I've conjured up every fantasy I can think of and turned it into real life.

"You look beautiful," he says.

Wow. How's that for changing the subject? I smile and stare at my hands. This is definitely a dream.

"Even when you blush."

It only makes me turn redder. I can feel it, my cheeks and nose, all warm.

"You'd think a girl like you would be used to compliments."

Yeah, not so much. No one ever notices me long enough to compliment me.

But somehow Connor is sitting here right now, and he sees me.

And I think I could get used to it.

August 30
ONE YEAR

When I awaken, the room is completely dark. The storm has lessened some, enough so that I can almost see the street lamps through the streaming raindrops on the window. I wait for a long moment, but the lightning doesn't come.

I wonder if he will return.

I wonder if the world still exists outside this room. I wonder if everybody else out there still remembers how to laugh. My smile is broken. It shattered a long time ago.

How long ago was it? Was it the first harsh word? The first bitter smirk or the first time he shoved me?

I close my eyes and push it away. It's over now. What's

done is done, and why it happened—or when—is inconsequential.

It won't change anything if I figure it out, anyway. Connor is who he is, and no matter how many ways I look at it, he still hurts me.

This isn't love. It's something broken and ugly. I wanted it so badly I didn't care what it looked like.

He did this to me. He chose to do it. Maybe he's broken and maybe he needed an outlet, but he still had a choice. He knew when he threw his fist what he was doing.

He knew when he spit those ugly words what they would do to me.

And I hate myself for hoping he's still in the parking lot, for wanting to open the door and let him back in.

I'll never be the person I was before him. But I don't have to be this girl, either.

With my left hand, the only piece of me not pulsing with pain, I reach into my pocket. My cell phone. When I flip it open, it lights up so brightly I have to blink several times before I can see clearly.

I have to do it. I have to call.

With shaky hands, I dial her number. I stop on the last digit, my finger hovering over the five. I don't know if I can do this. I don't know if I want to talk to her, to know that she's thinking *I told you so* and hating him.

She is harder to face than he is, even when his features are contorted into an ugly mask of rage. She is the proof of every wrong choice I made. When I look at her, I want to crawl into a hole and forget all the mistakes.

But I can't stop myself. I push the number anyway. I know she's not going to wrap me up in her arms and tell me everything is going to be okay, but I still want her to.

Somewhere inside me, I am still twelve years old, and I still need her.

I know she's sleeping. I know the phone will ring out with its shrill tone from the place beside her bed.

"Hello?" she answers, in a groggy voice on the second ring.

"Mom?" I don't realize I'm crying until I say that word, and it comes out so weak and wobbly it belongs to a child.

"Ann? Is that you?" She's awake now. Her voice is clear, filled with concern and, maybe, hope.

She wants it to be me on the line. Does she miss me like I miss her? Does she feel that distance between us—not caused by one year of fighting, but several years of silence?

The tears are pouring, sliding down my cheeks and dripping to the floor. I can't stop them.

"Come get me," I say, my lip quivering. I'm shocked at the surge of relief I feel as I say the words; I'm surrendering control.

Save me. Please, just make this all go away.

For a long second she doesn't say anything. The buzz of the phone is deafening. My heart flips around for a moment. Have I made a mistake? Is she too angry about the last twelve months?

"Ann?"

"Yeah?" I can hardly speak with the lump in my throat. It's choking me.

"I love you."

I can't even say it back, because those three words just make me sob even harder.

I am going to be okay.

I don't know what is going to happen next, but somehow, even after the year I've been through, I am going to be okay.

August 30
THE FIRST DAY

My car won't start. This is lame.

And *so* not good timing, considering I drained my cell phone while talking to Abby during lunch break, and I already set the alarm at Subway. If I go back in to use the phone, the alarm company will call and I'll have to tell them why I went back inside, and then tomorrow I'll have to explain it all to my boss.

Today has not been a good day. I only work here during the summer, and for some reason everyone thinks that summer equals Subway, because I didn't stop moving for six hours and the oven was cranked so we could keep up with baking the bread, and at one point the thermostat said it was ninety-nine degrees inside.

Ugh. Now I'm sweaty and tired and I just want to go home, but no, I had to leave my lights on and now I'm sitting here, trying to figure out what to do. I don't even have jumper cables to use, if someone had a running car.

So ... plan B. My car is a stick shift. The parking lot is pretty flat, but maybe I can get it going enough to push-start it. I'll get it rolling, and then I'll jump into the seat, put it in gear, and pop the clutch. It's worth a shot, since I have nothing else to do. It doesn't have to roll that fast. Hopefully.

So I jump out and lean against the door frame, but the car hardly budges. It's like there are blocks under the tires or something. I strain a moment longer, shoving with all my weight, but it doesn't roll an inch.

This is not going to work. I'm way too tired for this crap. Maybe I can get my cell to work long enough to call Abby and she'll come get me. She won't know how to use jumper cables and neither do I, but she can give me a ride home and I can deal with this on a day when I'm not so exhausted.

"Need a hand?"

I whirl around to see a boy standing there. He's probably around my age. Maybe a year older. He has spiky blond hair and a tall lanky body, like a basketball player or something. He's got on wide-legged blue jeans, the front all faded, and a plain black T-shirt, with a silver chain necklace hanging over the front.

And he's cute. Really, really cute. He has thick lips that sort of curl up a little bit, so it's hard not to stare at them.

And I'm standing here like a total tool, trying to push-start my own car. Great.

"Um, yeah. I left my lights on all day and so I was going to push-start it, but I can't really get it going."

"I have jumper cables, if you want. Or I can push you."

I nod my head and then realize he didn't ask a yes or no question. "Oh, um, yeah, jumper cables are fine."

He turns and walks away from me, and for a second I think I might have scared him off and he's just leaving. But then I see he's climbing into a big white truck over by the pizza place. He fires it up and drives it next to my little blue car.

It takes me almost five minutes to figure out where the hood release is, my hand blindly swiping across everything under the steering wheel, but I manage to pull it and before I can even say or do anything he's popping it open and attaching the clamps, and we both just stand there, staring at the engines.

"Give it a second, okay?" His voice is kind of rough-edged and masculine, and I find myself liking the sound of it and wishing he had more to say.

I sit down at the curb, reveling in the fact that I'm off my feet for the first time in hours. They actually throb. I close my eyes and rest my chin on my knees, my eyes closed for just one second.

"Rough day?"

I look up at him to see him leaning against my car, his arms crossed in a way that makes them look much bigger than they did when he walked up. He's kind of built.

"Yeah. Just a long one, really."

"Guess no one wants hot food on a day like this. They all want sandwiches. But none of 'em want to make them."

For a second I wonder how he knows that I make sandwiches, and then I realize my ugly purple polo shirt says *SANDWICH ARTIST* right on it, like that's a real occupation or something. Why does it have to say something so stupid?

"Yeah. I only have to do this gig for another week and then once school starts, I'm off the hook." I wipe some bread crumbs off my polo shirt and try not to wince at the fact that I have a big stripe of bright yellow mustard down the front.

"Sweet."

"Uh-huh." I wish I had something intelligent to say, something to show him I'm not just some idiot who leaves her lights on all day and accessorizes with mustard, but nothing comes to mind.

He just keeps leaning against the fender of my car, looking equal parts relaxed and hot. Or maybe it's just a severe case of knight-in-shining-armor.

"So, you live around here?" I ask.

"Yeah. By Larriot Park. You?"

I nod. "Yeah. On Snob Hill."

He laughs. It sounds beautiful. "I didn't think you guys called it that. I thought it was just us little people."

I grin. "Well, my neighbors would probably hate me if they heard me call it that, but I don't care. They're all snobs." I grin at my joke, and he smirks back, and I finally feel like I've said something worthy of conversation. "But at least my room has a nice view of the ocean," I add.

He nods and looks at the cables again, as if he can tell by sight when they've done their job. "Okay, give it a try."

I get up from the curb and walk over to my car, trying hard not to glance back to see if he's checking me out and wishing just as much that he is. I slide into my little bucket seat, say a few Hail Marys, and try it. For a second I think it's going to work, but just before it turns over, it dies again and starts clicking.

I butt my head into the steering wheel a few times in frustration. I just want this to work, because this guy has to think I'm a total idiot by now and he'll probably bail on me at any minute.

"Okay, give it a little while. You must have really drained it."

I go back and sit on the curb again, and he watches me, and I try to act like I don't notice.

So maybe this day doesn't totally suck. This hot guy is leaning over my car and trying to fix it for me. And I like the way he's confident but still has a charming, shy sort of smile.

Oh my God, I just called him *this guy*. I don't even know his name.

I stand up and walk over to him.

"My name is Ann, by the way." And then I awkwardly stick my hand out.

"Oh, sorry." He wipes his hand on his jeans and holds it out. "I'm Connor."

Interview

WITH AMANDA GRACE

In *But I Love Him*, you chose to tell the story backwards, beginning at the end, so to speak. Why do you feel it was the best way to tell Ann's story?

The structure of the novel has a lot to do with my purpose for writing the book. I wrote it because I wanted people to understand abusive relationships, and why the victims of domestic violence don't simply walk away. So often, a person thinks of themselves as too smart to end up in a similar situation. As the person reads, he or she chooses a defining moment (often the first time an abuser pushes or hits the victim) where they say to themselves, "that is when I would have left." From then on, they place a certain amount of blame on the victim for being in the situation in the first place.

By telling the story in reverse chronological order, it removes the reader's ability to judge the protagonist. They don't know the events that led up to the abuse, so they can only sit back and observe.

This book is a shift in tone from your previous teen novels, going to a very dark place. What inspired this story?

I was involved in a relationship when I was seventeen (Ann's age when she meets Connor) that, while not physically abusive, was intense and difficult, and became the inspiration for this story. I was only with this person for a year, but it had a profoundly deep impact on me, in much the same way Connor changes Ann. That's a big part of why Ann's relationship is exactly a year long.

I attempted to write a book like *But I Love Him* a few times, over the course of several years, but I never got beyond the first couple of chapters. Once I tried writing it in reverse chronological order, the dam broke, and the rough draft was done within a few weeks.

Connor is interesting because he's got a volatile temper and he abuses Ann both physically and psychologically. But we see that he's been treated that way all his life as well. We may sympathize with his background but not condone his behavior and actions. How did you achieve that balance?

I've read several YA novels about abusive relationships, and I didn't feel like any of them capture it just right. The problem is, the abuser in those books simply has an "anger problem." But domestic violence is about so much more than just someone's temper.

It was important to me that readers realize that Connor isn't a bad guy—just a very broken one. I spent a lot of time developing Connor's backstory, so that readers could understand what brought him to such a place. Truth be told, I'm a little nervous that people will be upset that he comes across sympathetic. My point isn't to make what he does seem okay, or even justifiable, but just to make it clear that there are deeply rooted problems here, far beyond anger management.

Abby, like Blake, serves as a reminder of Ann's previous life/previous self. She doesn't like Connor but for the most part she just lets Ann drift away from her. Did you ever consider having Abby discover the physical abuse? And if so, would she have been more assertive about intervening?

The thing with relationships—abusive or not—is that a girl never breaks up with her boyfriend because her friend doesn't like him. Abby is a smart girl, and she recognizes how deeply in love Ann is. While she may never explicitly confront Ann about the abuse, Abby has to know that something is very wrong with Connor and Ann's relationship.

Ann's mother takes the opposite approach—she tries almost constantly to push Ann away from Connor. But as you learn through the course of the novel, it only backfires—Ann has great difficulty, in the end, reaching out to her mother.

I guess my point is, you can't save someone who doesn't want to be saved. Abby knew that.

It's well known that abuse is cyclical (the abused often become abusers). Similarly, the abused can often find themselves in the same situations. Do you think Ann would do it all over again, knowing at the end what she does?

Sadly, I think it would depend on when you asked. A day, a week, a month after their relationship ends, she would probably say yes. But with time, distance, and a little perspective, I certainly hope she'd have the strength to say no.

You play with the idea of public and private selves in the narrative: Ann, Connor, even Ann's mother. Ann does a poor job maintaining her public self—it starts to deteriorate even though she manages to keep her biggest secret. Connor's private self (the good part of him, which Ann can see but no one else can) remains entirely private. Do you feel it's necessary for everyone to have these divided selves or would life be easier if we were all just one person?

I think it's human nature to have a public front and a private one, and what that truly means can vary widely from one person to the next. There are some people you can know your entire lives and never truly know them, and others seem to read like an open book. I think it has to be that way, though. Having a private side is a way to protect yourself from people who many not understand your innermost thoughts.

But that's why reading can be such an emotional, deeply moving experience—for a while, you live in someone else's head, and you see beyond their public self.

What can you tell us about your next book with Flux?

For now, all I'll say is that it revolves around a dark lie which spirals out of control.

Acknowledgments

My sincerest gratitude goes to my editor, Brian, for being smart, insightful, and insanely fun to work with; my agent, Zoe, who has been a true partner to me every step of the way; Courtney, Steven, Sandy, and the whole team at Flux for being Made of Awesome; and to Weronika, for plucking a little manuscript called *Shattered* out of the submissions stack, reading it overnight, and raving about it.